FIRST TO FAIL

UNRAVELED, BOOK 3

MARIE JOHNSTON

LE PUBLISHING

First to Fail

Copyright 2018 as Based on Principal by Marie Johnston

Editing by Razor Sharp Editing

Proofreading by My Brother's Editor and Double Author Services

Cover Art by Secret Identity Graphics

This is a work of fiction. Names, characters, places, and incidents are a product of the author's imagination. Locales and public names are sometimes used for atmospheric purposes. Any resemblance to actual people, living or dead, or to businesses, companies, events, institutions, or locales is completely coincidental.

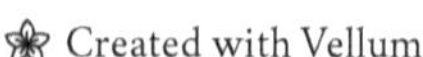 Created with Vellum

To the hubs.
You prove to me every day that I'm not exaggerating when I write
romance and stories with happily ever afters.

hris

"WELL, if DC Comics could make a solid movie, there wouldn't be so much complaining. It's not so much a DC versus Marvel thing as it is a long, boring movie thing."

I lifted my brow at the woman. Could she even be classified as a woman? She wore a costume that highlighted every curve, but her face looked all of eighteen. Since this was the Twin Cities Comic Con, she could be anywhere from fourteen to thirty-four. And dressed in skintight black vinyl and a red wig, she showcased the Marvel Universe fan craze. Her boyfriend sported a sleeveless black shirt, black tactical pants, and boots. He carried a bow and an empty quiver—no arrows with heightened security these days. They blended with the crowd of homemade cosplay costumes and Party City purchases.

Do not engage. But I couldn't let it go. "I don't know if it's so much the quality of the DC movies that's the issue." Which were excellent. Could they have been better? Yes. But did they deserve the many hours I spent defending them? A resounding no. "Marvel came out with some lesser characters and made them larger than life and hugely popular. But anyone old enough to walk was raised on Batman and Superman. They have their own ideas about what each one should be like, and they don't like their heroes messed with. Putting Henry Cavill in a blue skin suit with no red underwear on the outside was deeply upsetting for some."

At the actor's name, the girl's eyes glazed with dreamy desire. So she was, what, twenty to twenty-five? My fourteen-year-old daughter lost focus when I started discussing movies because she had zero interest in someone who wasn't young enough to be in a boy band.

The woman's saccharine smile grated. "At least they didn't put nipples on Iron Man's suit."

Always with Batman's nipples in *Batman and Robin*. That was an unfortunate rendition I never tried defending—and never confessed to enjoying.

The guy with the DC hater spoke, apparently needing to defend his own geek knowledge. It was probably very little, since I had never seen the guy shop at Arcadia, my comic book shop. "Who is that poster of anyway? Some knockoff of Batman?"

I made an effort to represent both major comic book universes equally, but not always with the box office headliner heroes. "No, he's a superhero in his own right."

"Who's that?" the girl asked, derision clear in her voice.

Why were they at my booth in the first place? Just to diss my display? Mara and I had run a booth at the local comic con since we'd opened shop, back when Arcadia used to be solely hers. When it had been shut down, I'd cashed in my IRA and proposed a partnership.

Here we were, bigger than last year, our booth gaining in

popularity. Mara and her husband handled the fans and customers while I dealt with insults. I didn't care why people dressed up or who they dressed as, but I wouldn't tolerate asshats putting down other fans.

I was about to explain who Nightwing was—how could I not?—when a woman beat me to it. "Why don't you watch *Teen Titans* and see if you still have questions?"

How could a voice drive a kick of lust through me like that? I wouldn't mind that voice lecturing me all night long.

Unlike the girl with the unsavory attitude, this stranger was all woman. Dressed in a skin-hugging maroon suit that revealed a tight body and mouthwatering curves, she stood with her hands on her hips, like a real superhero who'd just landed and was assessing the situation. Her pitch-black hair was obviously a wig, but better quality than what we sold in Arcadia. The mask covering half her face let my imagination wander about the extent of her beauty, but her pursed lips and strong chin were stern and sexy—especially because she wasn't putting up with the couple trashing comic book fans.

"Why would I do that?" the girl asked, her tone snotty.

"Because you'll find out who Nightwing is and can come to your own conclusions about what you think instead of bowing to popular opinion."

The girl rolled her eyes. "What are you supposed to be anyway, or am I supposed to read that somewhere, too?"

The stunner in maroon smiled and kicked a hip out. "I am my own creation. Valaria the Assassin at your service."

I grinned. Normally I didn't mind the questions, the discussions, or even the arguments. I relished them. It was the tone of this couple I couldn't stand. And Valaria the Assassin had slain it.

"You do you," the girl said and towed her guy away from the booth.

I heaved a sigh of relief and met Valaria's gaze. Her eyes

were such a dark brown that they had to be contacts. She embodied her deadly character from head to toe, except for her grin. Whoa…was that a dimple peeking out from under her mask? Valaria went from deadly sexy to adorable with a few facial muscles.

"I hate that phrase," she said, but she was still smiling.

I'd forgotten everything before looking at her. "What phrase?"

"'You do you.' It's been twisted into a coward's way out of an argument by hurling the ball into the other person's court without giving them a chance to take a shot."

I wasn't prepared for the depth of conversation my absent question prompted. We'd gone from discussing a superhero to society's tendency to shun conflict. My daughter said "you do you" at least once a day.

"Yeah. Totally agree." I had no clue what I was agreeing to, only that I didn't want Valaria to leave. A glance down the booth revealed we were in a lull. A new round of workshops had started and taken a load of attendees off the show floor. Mara was chatting with one of our regulars, and her husband was getting drooled over by a gaggle of scantily clad girls.

Valaria followed his gaze. "Does he need saving, too?" She cocked her head, the ends of her long black hair brushing her breasts. "Maybe not. The girls look ready to melt down."

"Nah. That's my business partner next to him. She likes to watch her husband suffer."

Valaria's lips quirked. "Do they always dress like a superhero pair?"

"Yes. I told them they should start doing hero and nemesis."

The tinkle of Valaria's laugh was almost lost in the din of the room. People had filtered out, but it didn't take much for noise to echo off the walls and ceiling.

Valaria leaned over the table to scowl at his jeans and gray Henley. "Do you dress up?"

"I had to make do with a poster." I gestured to the one the couple had been teasing me about. "It was a rough morning."

I'd told Jaycee to wash my costume, and she'd tossed it into the dryer on high heat. I'd have to regress to prepubescence if I ever wanted to fit into it again.

"A rough morning is a sign of unpreparedness." The light note in her tone took the bite out of her words.

"Or of having a teenage daughter."

She laughed again. "I don't have kids, but I work at— Are you married, too?"

Her abrupt change in course took me off guard and spurred unwelcome memories of Jaycee's mother. If I'd had my wish, I would've tied the knot long ago. "I haven't had the pleasure. You?"

"No, I usually scare my dates off long before the marriage stage."

I laughed. That should be a warning, but I liked her honesty. "You or Valaria?"

Her chuckle was just as easy, like we hadn't cut to the chase on our attraction: *You married? No, you? Nope. Wanna date?*

Well, we hadn't gotten that far, but I wanted to. Valaria was too interesting to let disappear into the myriad of anime characters and superheroes wandering around.

"If I don't, whipping out the Valaria outfit usually does. It's hard to find a guy who gets the whole cosplay thing."

"Ditto on the dating side. Or I find someone a little too zealous. I own a comic book shop and I usually dress the part for comic cons, but I don't wash dishes or clean the bathroom with my cape on."

"You're doing it wrong, then."

"Maybe that's the problem. I'll try it next time."

She grinned and even through her dark contacts, her eyes twinkled. "Does your daughter join in on the fun?"

Wasn't that a whole different topic. "She used to. And she's out of the worst of her 'God, Dad, you're so embarrassing stage,' but she's moved on to the fiercely independent stage." And the guy she liked wasn't a fanboy, so she was shunning all things masks and secret identities these days.

I hoped she got over that stage quickly. I wanted my fun-loving, quick-witted daughter back, not the stiff girl who felt the eyes of the world judging her.

"In my experience, if it doesn't have an ROI, it's not worth doing for some teens. And the incentive isn't always monetary."

I considered her words. Valaria was right. I'd asked, but I hadn't thought of the comic book shop as a form of employment. Arcadia was mine. I'd given up my other career for Jaycee. Was I expecting father-daughter time to be enough of a benefit to entice Jaycee to work at Arcadia?

Valaria glanced around. "Any other booths you recommend? I've never been to this comic con before. None of the current workshops interest me, but I don't want to leave yet."

I didn't want her to leave either. The crowd had filtered out, and Mara and Wes were next to each other with their heads bent in together, probably discussing how the morning had gone. Mara and I would talk later, but they both valued Wes's business insight.

My stomach grumbled. I barely had enough time to inhale breakfast. "Have you been to the food trucks?" When she shook her head, I seized my chance. "Want to grab a bite?"

"If you're certain I won't poison you. It's one of my methods, you know."

"Since I'm an ordinary guy today, it depends on you. Villain or hero?"

"Everyone thinks I'm a villain, but I'm really the hero, taking out what they don't know is bad for them." Her lips quirked.

Sounded like being a dad. I turned to Mara. "Hey, you two mind if I take an hour?"

Mara's gaze jumped from me to Valaria. Wes's brow cocked in a *you go, bro* way. "Wes and I can handle it."

I didn't have anything to bring with me, so I circled around the booth. Valaria and I walked to the show floor's exit.

"So, what's your name?"

She peeked up at me. Her mask molded to her face. It was quality crafted, like the rest of her suit. Like the rest of the body underneath it. "I was just going to be Valaria today, but I'll make an exception for you. Natalia, and Valaria really will kill you if you call me Nat."

"Natalia." The name was as unearthly sexy as she was. What was her real hair color? Her brows were penciled in dark despite being mostly covered by the mask. It showed her level of dedication to her costume. Where had she purchased it? We could stock the brand in Arcadia. "Natalia? Were your parents…?"

"Marvel fans? Most definitely not. Black Widow is nothing more than a spider to my father."

"Mine aren't into this stuff either. I got into it because they were always working, and I watched TV and read comics."

"Ah, the most popular babysitter ever: television." Again, her tone was light as she touched on another deep topic. What did this woman do for a living? "Rather, the most popular of *our* day. Now it's the smartphone."

"Yeah, but I've had better luck trusting electronics than some of the babysitters I've hired in the past."

Laughter burst from Valaria. "I believe it."

The greasy smells of tacos in a bag and deep-fried cheese curds wafted down the hall. Beyond the propped-open doors, a section of the parking lot had been roped off for a variety of food trucks. Valaria didn't look like a funnel cake girl, but I was hungry enough to gnaw on a turkey leg all afternoon.

"This is like a street fair." Valaria gaped at the multicolored trailers and tents.

"Pick your poison. Thai, Greek, Midwestern…Renaissance."

She giggled and clasped her hands together. "This is fabulous. Whose idea was it to combine a comic con with a food truck fair?"

She was asking rhetorically, but I was on the planning committee. I could mention it, but I didn't want to come off as boasting. Most of the time, I was grateful one of my ideas panned out, but her awe didn't stop my ego from swelling to superhuman size.

"Whatcha in the mood for?" I couldn't help how my gaze dipped to her mouth. I was hungry but looking at how her body moved in that latex outfit could satiate me for a few hours.

She caught me looking. With her mask, I could hardly tell if her brows arched, but the corners of her lips lifted. Not a full smile, but close enough to keep me from being mortified. The last thing I wanted was to scare her away.

It'd been a while since I interacted with a woman who wasn't a customer in the store. I was off my game and lacking any of my old charm.

"I didn't come here for the company or the food, but I think I'm pleased with how both have turned out." She went back to scanning the food trucks. "A gyro sounds like it won't clog my arteries after two bites."

I spotted the vendor offering Greek fare. "I'll join you. I've never had one."

"I've had one in Greece. Never from a parking lot," she said wryly and started for the truck.

"I would love to travel someday." We got in a line three people deep. The workshops hadn't ended yet, otherwise the wait would be twenty minutes or more just to order. "I was technically a kid when my daughter was born, and any extra cash went to her and her mother."

I hadn't meant to be that bluntly honest, but when it came to being a single parent and dating, full disclosure was best. I learned the hard way.

When I'd finally had the funds to travel, Jaycee's mother had decided she couldn't handle being a mom, and I'd been promoted to full-time dad. I'd quit my lucrative job to find something where I could be around for my daughter.

"I've traveled my entire life. It came with my family, I guess." She hadn't said what her last name was. What would go with Natalia? "Oh my god, they make their own flatbread? I wish I could eat here all week."

We reached the window and put in our order. She extracted some cash from a well-concealed pocket before motioning to me to add my order to hers.

"No, my treat." I'd never had a date pay before, but I hadn't been on a date in…too long. Since I'd always been the one asking, I'd always paid, and technically, I'd asked today, too.

She waved my offer off. "I think I can spare a twenty."

I didn't protest and added my order to keep from insulting her. We moved to the side to wait for our food with the people who'd ordered before us.

A chance meeting had morphed into a pseudo date. I could get used to this. "You saved me earlier, now you're buying my food. You're gonna think I'm taking advantage of you."

Natalia smirked. "You don't strike me as that type of guy. Valaria has a good sense of character."

When our food was ready, we made our way to one of the picnic tables set up on the far end of the parking lot. The convention center blocked any wind, the sun was out, and even though it was October, the temperature was mild. Sweater weather—or skintight maroon latex weather.

As we ate, we people watched, discussing costumes and outfits, and guessing at the origins of the more unique cosplay characters. Like me, Natalia had watched every episode of *Face Off*. Her laughter was one of the best sounds I'd ever heard. Given the heavy topics she'd touched on earlier and the way she would clear her throat and stare down at her plate after a giggle, I suspected she didn't laugh often. It was like her mirth caught her off guard.

What was the real color of her eyes? The answer to the question seemed more critical as our time wound down.

What did my sexy assassin really look like? If she was as stunning as her personality, I was a goner.

A group of teenagers walked by and Natalia inspected them, her eyes narrowed. A moment later she dismissed them like she hadn't recognized any of the kids.

She ate with her mask in place. Natalia No Last Name. But I couldn't fault her for not opening up to me and giving me free access to her life story like the top flap of a comic book. I had taught Jaycee not to give away all her personal details to the first guy who showed a little interest.

Our meal was over too soon, and I had to get back to work. I grabbed our wrappers and took them to a garbage can. When I turned, she was right behind me. We walked back to the entrance to the convention hall.

"When can I see you again?" I asked as soon as we got inside.

Just then, the doorways to two conference rooms opened and people with robes and capes—and the occasional plain street clothes—flooded out. I hooked Natalia's arm and pulled her around the corner. The bathrooms were in the opposite direction, making this part of the conference center relatively private.

I stopped to face her but looked over her shoulder to see if we were going to get interrupted. Foot traffic was going in a different direction and we were mostly isolated. I looked back at her. Her lips parted as she gazed up at me.

I had one question—*what's your phone number?*—but I couldn't ask it. I wasn't worried about calling her when I had her in my arms.

Her eyes were hooded and she leaned closer. I closed the gap, drawn to her like a magnet I was helpless to resist, and dropped my lips onto hers.

A soft gasp escaped her, but she rose to her tiptoes, her hands coming around my shoulders for support. Winding my arms around her tight waist, I marveled once again over how well her outfit encased her body. I could feel every inch of her, but she was fully clothed. The warm fabric was smooth under my hands, allowing me to enjoy the solid curves of her body.

I deepened the kiss, and she opened for me. A strong, take charge woman like this let me lead? I'd take every inch she allowed me, and I'd make sure we weren't interrupted. I backed us toward the cove outside of an unused conference room for extra privacy. With each step, her breasts rubbed through my shirt, the quality material not strong enough to suppress her peaked nipples.

Her tongue twined with mine, soft, hot, and needy. Blood left my head to pump to my groin until the fly of my jeans dug into my flesh. Natalia's warm body against mine, a subtle undulation against my erection, I was done. I gripped her ass and squeezed. What would this be like if we were naked? If just kissing her was this lust inducing, what would sleeping with her be like?

She rocked against me, her pelvis stroking my erection. We were both having the same fantasy of being alone together and sans costume. I wedged a knee between her legs, and she didn't hesitate. She ground against my thigh like it was her job and I was flinging fifties.

I took the kiss deeper, timing my tongue with her movements and massaging her ass with my hands as her butt flexed and relaxed against my palms.

A moan escaped me, mingling with her heavier breaths. My only mission in life was to get her to come. Smashed together, feeling every inch of her body, it wasn't enough. I wanted her falling apart in my arms.

Loud voices and rowdy laughter approached.

She pulled back, a gasp ripping from her throat, and stumbled out of my arms. Lifting her hand to touch her kiss-swollen lips, she shook her head. "I'm…I should be…I don't usually move this fast. I'm new in town, and jumping into some guy's arms…"

The dismay etched on her face cleaved through my lust. We just met, but this wasn't some fling to me. There's more to me and Natalia. I know it. "I'd like to be more than some guy. Are you free next weekend?" I didn't even know what she looked like, but I enjoyed her passion, and she was easy to talk to. Under that black wig and those dark contacts, Natalia outshone Valaria.

"I—" She adjusted her wig and scowled. Had it dawned on her, too, that I didn't know what she really looked like? Will that make it seem less significant to her? "I'm not ready to date. I just moved here and my job…"

I held my hands up. Her nerves were coiling tighter, her tension was almost palpable. "No pressure. We can exchange numbers and when you're free maybe we can grab supper or hit up a movie?"

I'd almost lost her until I said movie. Her eyes lit up. "I like movies." Her expression fell. "I left my phone in the car rather than have the outline of a rectangle on my ass."

The whole time I'd been feeling her up in that suit, I hadn't felt a phone. "Valaria doesn't have a friends-and-family account, huh?"

She chuckled. "No."

The reminder of her ass in that costume threatened to send more blood to my fading erection. She rattled off her number and I triple-checked it was stored before we walked back to the showroom floor.

I couldn't wait to see her again.

atalia

"Ms. Shaw?"

I looked up from my computer screen, schedules and change requests still emblazoned across my eyes. My young assistant's voice was hesitant, like she worried I would send her packing for the interruption.

I'd only done that to an assistant once during my first position after graduate school. Maybe twice. Being taken seriously as the principal of a private school when I'd just turned thirty and had little teaching experience wasn't easy. I stuck to being a hard-ass. The reputation stuck with me through to this position and I need to live up to it. Being brought on board to keep one of my father's schools from sinking was about stopping the abuse of power that had been dragging the school down, not being tough for no reason. I always had a valid reason.

"What is it, Ms. Branson?" I pushed away from the desk.

My assistant was nearly as new as I was. I had only arrived at the beginning of the month, but Ms. Branson had started a month earlier when the new school year had begun. I had kept her on because Ms. Branson had just turned in her resumé, disgusted with the atrocious behavior of the last principal. With at least one person in my corner, maybe I could save this ship from getting toppled by the next wave of parental outrage.

Just like I'd done at the previous school I'd fixed.

"The history teacher brought down a freshman. The girl was late for class all last week and Mr. Budinsky has had enough." Ms. Branson looked behind her, then stepped into the room, holding the door almost completely closed. "He's also tried disciplining her for abusing the use of his name."

Budinsky. I could imagine all the ways a teenage mind would twist that.

"Give me a few minutes. I'll let you know when to send her in." The girl's tardiness wasn't the major concern. It was what had caused her to arrive late to class. Again with the teenage mind.

I logged into the security footage. The cameras had been in disrepair, but they were one of the first things I had gotten fixed when I accepted the position of principal. The former principal had been sleeping with the head of the finance department and they'd redirected funds. Some had been embezzled, the rest diverted to bulk up the football team and purchase a new bus. Never mind that the library had one DVD player to check out and it was the first DVD player most of the school's students had ever seen.

Assuming the student was in the current period, I reviewed the security footage of the minutes before and after Mr. Budinsky's class started. It was only Monday and tardiness looked to be on the schedule for this week. The grainy footage of a girl sauntering up to the closed door, shooting a shit-eating grin over her shoulder, was clear enough. The student wore a khaki skirt, which wasn't popular with the girls. Most preferred pants, since leggings went against the dress code.

Preston Academy had a uniform dress code. Navy blue or khaki pants or skirts. Red, navy, or white polo shirts could be paired with them.

I punched into another camera's feed. A boy lingered in front of a storage closet. I narrowed my eyes. I'd never been in that particular closet, but I'd bet my father's new Audi that it had enough room for two kids to get handsy, especially if one of those kids wore a skirt.

"Not on my watch," I muttered. I sent Ms. Branson a message to send the student in. I also listed the camera and minutes for Ms. Branson to determine the identity of the boy.

Seconds later, my office door opened, and the girl slipped inside. Her light brown hair hung loose over wiry shoulders. Her light brown eyes were a rebellious mix of *do your worst* and *I don't care*. I might be deluding myself, but I thought I also saw a little *oh shit, what have I gotten myself into?*

I hoped the girl felt that way. It gave me a little hope that I could work with the student's behavior.

"Ms. Shaw." The girl sat primly in a chair on the other side of my desk. She looked around the office.

Yep, it was bare. I had spent the first week packing the former principal's trophies in a box. Then I'd loaded all the outdated textbooks and taken the haul to the end of the drive that led to Preston Academy. The old employee—or his mistress, who no longer worked at Preston Academy either—could come pick up his belongings as long as they didn't step foot on campus.

As for my decorating efforts, I'd find appropriate decor. My preferences had to go out the window. Movie posters and pop culture art were not appropriate for the head of a private school. I could just imagine the president of the school board wandering in and questioning his hiring choice.

I'd never been able to openly display the few knickknacks I'd collected over the years or the purchases I'd made at cons. But I'd been deliciously distracted from buying anything at the Twin Cities Comic Con.

I couldn't think about him now—or ever. I had no time for dating. Once my stint at Preston was done, I was off to fix the next academy. Because that's who I was: a fixer. To take my mind off my make-out session, I concentrated on the task at hand.

"Jaycee, why were you late for history?" I preferred to be direct. I wasn't these kids' BFF, and I wasn't going to act like it. It was my job to make sure they got a quality education while building respectable character. Chitchat didn't always fit into the equation.

"It takes too long to get from my locker to the classroom."

Some days it was hard not to say bullshit out loud. Preston Academy was a university prep school that was small enough to be all in one building. Built sixty years ago, it was solid brick like it belonged on a prestigious college campus, and only one addition had been added over the years. My grandfather's vision had never been to grow so large they needed to keep adding on. He insisted on quality over quantity. Until my father had taken over. It had cost me a ton of friendships and any popularity whatsoever because of all the moving. He'd gone on to build five more similarly sized campuses all over the country. Rich people wanted superior education for their kids and the more limited it was, the more prestigious it felt.

A message popped up on my screen. I read it, my heart

sinking to my Captain America–decaled toenails. "Who's Dresden Wentworth?"

My heart thumped in time with the flare of Jaycee's eyes. *Yes, I know who you've been making out with.* Unfortunately, my time going through records after starting this job also meant I knew the Wentworths were one of the biggest benefactors of the school.

The downfall of many private schools: those who gifted their money thought it came with strings attached. *Look, I just wrote a check for a hundred thousand and we need a quarterback with a solid arm. I just happen to know a student we can recruit for a full ride.*

I couldn't blame them. The sums paid for tuition and that were donated outright were staggering. But balance was needed between academics and extracurricular activities and that wasn't always appreciated. Retaining quality staff meant spending money on them, and some of their donors didn't understand the correlation.

"Dresden's a friend." Jaycee's gaze flicked away. "Why are you bringing him up?"

"He's a friend you've been late to history for. And it's something I need to inform your parents about." I glanced at the new message on my screen.

Jaycee lived with only one parent, her father. Her mother was listed as an emergency contact only.

I slid my gaze back to the girl. Issues at home then. Mom was out of the picture and Dad was either too strict or his little angel did no wrong.

Jaycee scowled at the top of my desk. "Do what ya gotta do."

Oh, I would. "Why do you call Mr. Budinsky names?"

The girl snorted. "Because he refuses to use my proper name. Until he does, I'm not using his proper name."

"What wrong name is he using?"

Jaycee gathered her hair and draped it down her back. What I wouldn't give to wear my hair down someday. But as the daughter of the man in charge of all six Preston Academies, I had to look as professional as humanly possible. Sharp suits, bound hair, and, when the occasion called for a little more flair, dark-rimmed glasses. I wore little makeup besides a brush or two of mascara and clear lip gloss. Dying my hair wasn't an option, thanks to the dress code, but I'd accumulated quite an assortment of wigs for my cosplay.

"He keeps calling me Ms. Halliwell when it should be Ms. Richards."

Richards? I glanced at the computer again. Ah. The mother's name.

"What's your legal name?" It had to be Halliwell. The school required legal names, not first preferences and not nicknames.

"Well," Jaycee fisted the cuffs of her long-sleeved emerald shirt, "Halliwell is on my birth certificate, but I went by Richards for years until…" Her gaze slid to the ceiling, then bounced to the wall. And there it was. The pain that made Jaycee act out. Textbook.

"Until you moved in with your father?"

Jaycee nodded but didn't meet my gaze.

"How are things going, living with him?"

"Fine. He's around a lot now. Like, *all* the time."

"He never used to be?" Half of my job called for being a counselor. Preston Academy had one on staff, but I wanted to learn about Jaycee before I shuffled the girl's case off.

Jaycee crossed her legs. One or both of her parents must be tall. I had topped out at five foot five. My mother was two inches shorter and my father three inches taller. But I'd learned from both of them how to walk with swagger and an air of entitlement.

"No. Dad used to be a suit guy. Long hours, killer pay. But

when he got me, he quit to be home more. Now he works at…" Her gaze cut away. "When's he gonna be here?"

"In a few moments. Would you rather wait with Ms. Branson?" That'd give me some time to watch more footage and read Mr. Budinsky's entire report.

The girl sauntered out, her shoulders rounded in and her steps not as cocky as when she'd entered.

Was there trouble at home or unresolved issues with her mom's absence?

Several minutes ticked by. I scanned each day of the previous week. It was a daily occurrence. A quick disappearance into the closet until five minutes past the bell. Jaycee would creep out first and then Dresden would strut out like he didn't have a care in the world.

So why hadn't he been sent to my office? I looked up his schedule. My stomach sank.

If I were a superhero swooping in to save the school, Dresden's fifth-period teacher would be my nemesis. An evil villain who also happened to be the athletics director: Sam Samuelson. Coach Sammie, beloved by all the check-writing, former-jock parents.

"Fuck me," I muttered and jumped in my seat when someone rapped on the door. "Yes?"

Ms. Branson peeked in. "Mr. Halliwell is here. Would you like me to send them both in?"

"Just Mr. Halliwell first." It'd give me a chance to gauge his reaction. Sometimes parents talked more openly when their kids weren't around.

Ms. Branson stepped inside, and I rose to greet Mr. Halliwell. I was stepping around my desk when he cleared the doorway. I stopped short and my thigh bumped the edge of the desk. Pain shot through my leg, but I gritted my teeth against a curse word.

The man I had twined myself around not two days ago at the comic con had just entered my office.

Chris was Mr. Halliwell? He was dressed nearly identically to when I'd met him. There was no denying he was the same person I'd dry humped.

I'd made out with a student's parent?

Mortification swept through me. The one time I'd lowered my guard, and I'd committed professional suicide. I'd come here as the ballbuster to knock the place back into shape. If those who resisted my efforts found out I had a personal relationship with a student's father, they would double down to undermine me.

He smiled, that easy grin I'd dreamed about each night since the convention, but it was filled with tension. "Hello, Ms. Shaw."

He didn't recognize me. Gone was the black wig, leaving my shoulder-length honey brown hair wound tightly in a bun. Gone were my contacts. He wouldn't have been able to tell my eyes were hazel, more on the brown side than green, under the contacts. And thanks to my father's dental plan, I didn't have chipped teeth, gaps, a gold cap, or any other identifiable feature in my mouth.

Had I evaded social destruction? "Hello, Ch—Mr. Halliwell." I stomped around the desk to give him a firm handshake, trying to forget his hands had been on my ass, squeezing and rubbing. I gestured to the seat Jaycee had vacated and scurried back to my own.

He glanced around the office. It was what everyone did when they first sat down. Of course, his gaze landed on the single prism I'd set on the shelf. It was the shape of Superman's emblem, but when I turned it a certain way, no one could tell. It was the one geeky adornment I allowed myself. If anyone mentioned it, I could fake ignorance.

"Okay, Mr. Halliwell, let me get to the point of why we

called you here." I gave him the rundown of Jaycee's tardiness, made him aware of her last-name angst, and outlined the consequences.

And I did it all without my voice shaking and without staring at his lips. Good. It was time to shove the case file off to the counselor. Now that I had his number from Jaycee's file, I could make sure I never answered if he tried to call.

hris

IT WAS hard to take my eyes off Ms. Shaw. "I'm sorry. Have we met before?"

Her bright gaze pierced me like she had laser vision. The rest of her wasn't any less severe. Did she get a headache from binding her hair so tightly? Did she ever smile?

She was probably stunning when she smiled.

She sure wasn't smiling now. "I don't believe so."

I cleared my mind of all things attractive about Ms. Shaw. Like how her skirt wrapped snuggly around her hips when she circled her desk, or how round her ass was. A guy could—

Yeah, those things. That was what I needed to clear. I was in the principal's office for my daughter.

I wished it was the first time. No, I wished there was no first time, but I'd been on a first-name basis with all of

Jaycee's principals. This was my first time at Preston Academy, but only because it was her freshman year.

What was Ms. Shaw's first name? Was it sturdy like Gertrude? Or ethereal like…Natalia?

I couldn't think about her right now. Never had two women captured my attention so securely and done so fully clothed while speaking frankly.

I couldn't be pondering Ms. Shaw when I planned to call Natalia tomorrow night. I'd been patiently waiting for the three-day window to pass so I wouldn't look too desperate before I called her. And since I counted Saturday as day one, that made today time to call. I didn't want to be forgotten.

I couldn't forget Natalia after that kiss.

Ms. Shaw's firm voice cut through my thoughts, her eyes hard. They were the brown of Gambit's trench coat, not too dark, not too light, but interspersed with green. I would've remembered her if we'd met before.

She described Jaycee's tardiness and the way she was acting out with one of her teachers. Again with the last name.

If only Jaycee's previous teachers had stayed firm, but too many of them had indulged her. The private school wouldn't, but they might fear my ex's parents' wrath. Their pocketbooks had more say than I did.

I processed everything she said about Jaycee and started with the most concerning. "Is there a limit to the amount of tardiness?"

"No." Ms. Shaw arranged a stack of papers that had already been in a tight pile. That was a good way to describe her office. Tight and tidy. Just like the woman.

My mind wandered to how the cut of her jacket highlighted her shoulders before it tapered down to her waist and flared at her hips. She wasn't a waif. Ms. Shaw hid her figure, but she couldn't hide her strength. What did she do for a workout?

I had to quit obsessing about a woman I'd just met…in favor of another woman I'd just met.

Was I that desperate to date again? My personal life had been slow since I'd left my career behind to be more available for Jaycee. It was hard to strike up a conversation with an intelligent, professionally successful woman that started with "I work in a comic book shop."

I never admitted to owning it. Would that even help? Certainly not when they found out the co-owner was married to one of the wealthiest men in the Twin Cities. Mara's husband didn't lend a financial hand, but he had connections that had saved Mara and I a lot of green when we'd been planning the store.

Arcadia was successful in its own right, but I wasn't about to sit and defend my current profession to get laid. But I doubted I'd ever find a woman who'd stick around long enough to find out.

"Let me rephrase my answer," Ms. Shaw continued. "There *is* a policy, but it's been sorely ignored and I'm updating it. Three times leads to detention, five leads to suspension, and more than five will result in expulsion."

My brows rose and my lust hid in a corner. Ms. Shaw wasn't fucking around. How was I going to get Jaycee through four years of high school?

Ms. Shaw snagged a pair of dark-rimmed glasses and shoved them on. Could she not see me or were they her form of armor? "Jaycee has earned two hours of detention, but combined with the other behavior, I was concerned enough to feel a visit with you was warranted. We'll settle on detention for now, but due to the number of issues, one more infraction and it'll be suspension."

When Jaycee had come home at the beginning of the month with news about a new principal and juicy gossip about the old one, I'd been nothing more than mildly interested. Then she'd come home after Ms. Shaw's first day complaining about what an iron maiden she was. I'd asked Jaycee if she'd say the same thing about a male principal. An eye roll had been my only answer.

The last principal hadn't impressed me. During orientation, the guy had worked the parental crowd like a life-insurance salesman. He was everyone's friend and the more you spent, the more privileges your kid got. I had hardly spoken to the guy.

"Perhaps it's time to bring Jaycee in." Ms. Shaw rose, and I reclined in my chair, trying not to feel like I was relaxing for the show.

That tight ass rounded the desk as she walked to the door to call in Jaycee. I jerked my gaze away. The short beige heels she wore were enough to make her butt wiggle and incite all kinds of fantasies. I hadn't seen an ass that great since… Well, since Saturday.

She returned to her desk and thankfully I was distracted by my daughter slumping into the seat next to me. We were a matching pair.

I looked at her with what I hoped was fatherly disappointment, but Jaycee only jerked her gaze to Ms. Shaw like, *am I right?*

And, yeah, I kinda wanted to fist-bump my daughter and say *dude, spot on.*

I directed my gaze back to the principal. She was coolly studying Jaycee. Dammit. But if Jaycee insisted on a lack of tact, she'd have to pay the consequences.

Which was why I was here.

Ms. Shaw shuffled the same stack of papers. Was that their only function? Instead of a stress ball, she had papers? "With detention, we offer two choices. All at once after school—I'm here until then and can supervise. Or one hour on two consecutive days. It'd start tomorrow."

Jaycee only had her permit, and the private school couldn't use a public school service bus. I usually left work to pick her up and she came to the store with me. She used to love it. Until this semester started.

"She'll do two hours tomorrow." I absolutely didn't make that decision to see Ms. Shaw again. I was confident lasting relationships didn't start with picking a kid up from detention.

Ms. Shaw lifted a brow at Jaycee. My daughter shrugged and avoided looking at me.

"About the name-calling—"

Jaycee cut Ms. Shaw off. "Oh my god. Mr. Budinsky's an adult, and he's getting snippy about a kid messing up his name?"

"Jaycee…" I hadn't intended to say more, but Ms. Shaw was gazing at me like she was waiting for me to finish. I scrambled to find an acceptable reproach. "It's about respect."

"Then he can respect what I want to be called. Yet he refuses to use Richards." She crossed one leg over the other and folded her arms. I knew that mutinous look, the one she wore when she refused to listen. A spear of dread went through me when she pinned Ms. Shaw with that look. "I mean what if people called you *Mrs.* Shaw and knew perfectly well you're not married?" I cringed at the way she stressed *not married*. It wasn't a death sentence to be single. "Or what if they called you Natalie instead of Natalia?"

I jerked my head to face Ms. Shaw. Natalia Shaw. What were the odds her name was the same as—

What were the odds her ass was as spectacular in a skirt as in a Valaria costume?

What were the odds I'd feel like we'd met before?

The odds were pretty damn good. She couldn't hide that mouth, just like she couldn't hide the poleaxed expression in her widened eyes. My daughter's principal, the woman I couldn't quit fantasizing about, was the same woman I'd held in my arms just days ago.

~

Natalia

Aʜ, hell. How had I thought I was going to get away with that? If my first name was more common, Chris might've still doubted whether we knew each other or not. But the moment recognition hit him was obvious, as his soft brown eyes and he sat back like he'd hit a force field. But invisible forces were for comic books, along with the thought that a mask or thick-rimmed glasses were an adequate disguise.

I forced myself to focus on the topic at hand. "I understand why you're upset, but the issue of your last name is between you and your father. It is Preston Academy's policy to address each student by their legal name. We don't use nicknames, nor will we accommodate a last name that is not your legal last name. If you wish to be addressed by a different name, it will need to be reflected on your birth certificate." It was why I was Ms. Shaw and not Ms. Preston. I'd suffered enough through prep school with that last name.

When I'd been groomed to take over for my father and fix his good ol' boy oversights, I'd legally changed my name.

"I wasn't exactly asked an opinion about my birth certificate," Jaycee said snidely.

"As I said, that is between you and your parents. Due to your current level of detention, further disuse of Mr. Budinsky's name will result in suspension and possibly expulsion." Usually, I looked the parents in the eye when I stated that consequence, but I couldn't right now.

Jaycee's eyes flew wide. "For saying Mr. Butt-in-ski once in a while? You can't be serious."

"Jaycee—" Chris's voice was more exasperated than a warning. I wanted to tell him that he was in charge, not Jaycee, but like the last name thing, that was between him and Jaycee. My concern was the girl's behavior at school.

"Dad!"

I cut in before the focus was taken off the more severe problem. "I'm taking into account the tardiness. Perhaps you need to think long and hard about how much you want a boy to affect your prep school time." Jaycee blinked at me. Nope. The girl hadn't thought of it like that before and she was attempting to control her environment left and right. From the way Chris's jaw clenched, he hadn't thought of it like that either. "It's a lot of power to give a boy when you'll be facing the repercussions."

"Jaycee, wait outside while I talk to Ms. Shaw."

I squirmed under his commanding tone. I'd only known him as easygoing. Today, he'd been almost defeated and sheepish, but now… At the moment, not even Jaycee argued with him.

Jaycee huffed out of her chair and stepped outside. Thanks to the easy-close hinges, the door didn't slam. How many students would've gotten detention just for that otherwise?

Chris lifted his gaze to mine. My heart hammered. "So. Turns out we've met."

"You can understand why I didn't confirm your suspicions."

A muscle jumped in his jaw. I'd almost nibbled that muscle the other day. I would've nibbled a lot more than that.

He glared out the window. "She's upset."

I blinked. I'd been prepared for him to pounce on my deceit, stay upset with me, but he'd moved on to the issues with Jaycee. Understandable, but… Well, I'd thought I'd made a bigger impression. Not that this was the time to dwell on it.

"Understandable." I wanted so badly to know what had happened between Jaycee's mother and him. Usually, I preferred not to know. Getting the general impression of what was going on at home was enough to understand the motivation behind the delinquent behavior. Beyond that, my priority was the school.

But I was insatiably curious about Chris.

He scrubbed a hand over his face, leaving his hair ruffled in the front. He didn't style his hair and it hung longer than the professionals I usually ran across. My teachers were clean-cut and adhered to a dress code. The guys I dated were suit men, with the uptight personalities to match their cinched ties.

Chris was…loose. Not sloppy, but relaxed. Nothing like the guys who'd caught my eye before. But the fire flashing in his gaze when that couple had been haranguing him had caught my attention faster than a speeding bullet. Put all of it together and he was the last guy I expected to be one of my students' parents.

"She's… She can't get kicked out of school." He leaned forward to rest his elbows on his knees. His jeans hugged his thighs, and *damn*. I'd felt his body plastered up against me Saturday. His Suicide Squad shirt hugged an impressive chest. And now I was envious of the polyester cotton blend.

He was watching me. *Quit lusting, Ms. Shaw. Valaria wouldn't back down if she was busted.* "Yes, well, I laid out what she has to do."

"I suppose you can't tell me the name of the boy."

Grateful he wasn't trying to force the issue, I shook my head. "I can assure you that I will also be having a discussion with him and his parents." And the teacher who hadn't reported Dresden Wentworth. "I can recommend not making him forbidden. That tends to make the other party more appealing."

Chris nodded. "Her grandparents would— If she got kicked out, they'd never forgive me. And they'd use it to…" He gave a helpless shrug and shot her a small smile. "She's third generation at Preston Academy."

Was it bad that it showed? In my experience, the kids whose families had a history with the school had what I'd come to call "entitlement syndrome." They should've tried growing up the kid of the school's founders. That sense of entitlement would've been knocked right out of them by the other students.

"It's clear she's working through stuff. I don't want to expel her."

"I know." He rubbed his eyes and sighed. "Did you buy that at Arcadia?"

A burst of alarm went through me when he pointed to her prism. "Yes, actually. Wasn't that the booth you were working at?" My cheeks flooded with heat at the reminder of our kiss.

"Yes. I work at Arcadia."

I cocked my head. How did a guy who worked at a comic book shop afford private school tuition? Preston Academy didn't do scholarships for students who couldn't propel them toward sports championships—and wouldn't as long as my father had a say.

He gave me a wry grin. "How does a single dad who isn't a lawyer, bank president, or international something or other send his daughter to school here?"

I chuckled. "Yes, I was wondering that."

"Her grandparents foot the bill. It was a concession they made when her mother gave up on raising her. I agree to send her here and they cover tuition and won't fight me for custody."

"But you're her father."

"Yep. But they're loaded and I was too naïve when I was younger. Look, I know I'm not winning Dad of the Year, but Jaycee would have free rein at their place. She'd have the same personality as her mother and lack the character to follow through with challenges when the going gets tough."

And if she got kicked out, they'd fight him and he wouldn't be able to keep Jaycee. Wouldn't that mess with her head more? To feel like her dad had given up on her, too?

"I'm sorry, Chris. I really am. We've been going through some growing pains. The schools have been successful, and they don't always attract the people with the best morals to run them. I'm the one they bring in to clean the place up. Part of that is assuring our standards are maintained. That includes discipline."

He watched me for a heartbeat. I shifted in my seat. His intense scrutiny created another flush under my collar that went south. How could I be getting turned on just from him looking at me—in my office!

"Natalia—Ms. Shaw." He said my first name like a caress. Did I look as panicked as I felt? "Can you let me know immediately if Jaycee even seems like she's going to have more problems? I really need to avoid a legal battle with her grandparents until she's graduated."

No favoritism. But instead of a rejection, I said, "Sure."

Was he my kryptonite? Seven years of strict ethics and I was caving to one plea from a guy who'd made my toes curl with a kiss.

Not that it could ever happen again. Some days, I hated my job.

Most days.

I glanced at the prism. "Um, Chris. People here don't know about my hobby."

"Cosplay?"

I adjusted my shoulders and my gaze darted to the door. "I'd like to keep it private. It's hard to be the boss when they think—"

"—you're a geek?"

Geez, that felt so wrong to admit. But I wasn't known to dress up for Halloween anymore. I did, Halloween or not. But no one knew about it.

"Yeah, I get that. You notice Jaycee wasn't at the convention helping me work the booth?"

"I'm surprised. With all the blockbusters, it's not as if being a fangirl or boy is the kiss of social death it used to be."

"My guess is that the boy making her late for class isn't into it."

Ah yes. At least he wasn't totally ignorant about the factors affecting her behavior.

He straightened, a mix of defeat and determination on his face. "I'd better get back. Mara's covering for me and we start getting busy once school lets out." His wry smile reminded me of Saturday when we'd chatted over gyros. "Not all kids are ashamed of their interests."

I squashed my dismay down and stood up. I was an adult who kept more secrets than an undercover agent, but he wasn't the type to slip a subtle dig in when I'd asked him to keep my secret. But then, how would I know? Talking to him for an hour and making out with him for two minutes weren't enough to determine his personality. All the other guys I'd dated had no issues dissing me.

I did a quick mental check that my hands weren't sweaty and then stuck one out. He clasped it, his grip strong but not harsh and his hand warm. The contact didn't last long. He didn't drop my hand like a lead paperweight; he let his own slip off so gently I almost lunged to grab it back.

I was the principal. My brain was screaming that a

student's dad was off-limits. But my body wasn't getting the message.

He towered over me by at least eight inches. My head would fit perfectly against his broad chest. As I gazed up at him, the blatant desire I'd seen when we first met was back. My memory was as sharp as a tack when it summoned the feel and taste of him. He was so close and it was just the two of us.

Shoving his hands into his pockets—to keep from sweeping me into his arms again?—he smiled. "I guess this means I shouldn't call you."

He could have dumped a cold glass of water on me. Reality crashed back. "Yes. It does." *Please call me.*

No.

Hold firm, Natalia.

How could more heat infuse his gaze? Was my internal struggle obvious?

"That's a shame." He went for the door but stopped with his hand on the knob and spoke low. "Nice to see you again, Valaria."

My breath caught and I wanted to run after him like a damsel in distress. I wanted him to strip me out of my costume inch by inch while he devoured my body—but that fantasy needed to be relegated to the forgotten zone. I couldn't be anything more to Chris than his daughter's principal.

hris

I RANG up customers as the store's Saturday game-day club wrapped up their afternoon. Saturdays and Sundays were always busy days but some of my favorites. It might be the weekend, but it beat sitting through tag-team board meetings Monday through Friday. And I didn't have to work every weekend. Only when Jaycee was with her grandparents.

Work didn't stop me from thinking about *her*. Uptight Ms. Shaw turned Valaria the Assassin. Or vice versa? Was the real Natalia Shaw somewhere in the middle?

How many cold showers had I taken to get her transformation out of my mind? Uptight Ms. Shaw got me as hot as Valaria. I'd be in trouble if trouble was even an option. The way Ms. Shaw had booted Jaycee out of detention when I'd driven up the circular drive to the entrance of the school, she wasn't harboring aspirations of sneaking in forbidden time with me.

Glad to see the cosmic balance of my life was holding up.

Lose my virginity at seventeen, have a baby. Hit my career stride, become a single dad. Meet the woman of my dreams, discover she's my daughter's principal.

The game-club players started filing out. A few stayed behind to browse the aisles. They were all regulars and it'd been hours since lunch. I ducked to the back office to guzzle a water and check my messages.

My mouth twitched when I opened the picture Jaycee had sent. She was strolling behind her grandparents at the Mall of America. She had her tongue sticking out and her hand in the *rock on* position. I could make out the designer plush coat her grandmother was wearing and the tweed suit of her grandfather. They made an odd, but expensive pair. Add Jaycee and her torn jeans into the mix and no wonder Jaycee was blowing off steam, though it was in a thankfully subdued and not outrageous way.

It was the weekend Jaycee dined with her mother. At least Cierra was making an effort to stay in Jaycee's life, even if she refused to take any responsibility for the girl otherwise. Since Cierra did whatever her parents wanted, I probably should thank them.

But they never thanked me for a thing, so…

The bell for the front door dinged. I tossed my empty bottle in the recycling bin and strode back out and around the corner. Stopping, I stared at the new customer.

Natalia browsed through the action figure selections. Her eyes were narrowed and she was leaning close to the hanging display. My lips quirked. She was inspecting the detail on the figures for ideas. Was she coming up with a new character or expanding on Valaria?

This version of Ms. Shaw was better than the rest. She wore an emerald-green sweatshirt that I'd bet my collector comic book stash was a Preston Academy sweatshirt. Soft jeans molded her legs like Valaria's suit. On her feet were ballet slippers, and the best part? Her hair was down. No wig. No bun wound so tight that if the band snapped it could take out someone's eye. A cascade of light brown waves fell across the hood of her sweatshirt. My fingers twitched to run through it.

I had it bad.

She adjusted the tote over her shoulder and turned to scan the rest of the store. Had she been in here before? Yes, she'd bought the prism on her bookshelf. The lone object decorating her office, and I was probably the only person in the school who knew what it was. Well, me and Jaycee, but my daughter would never admit her knowledge in Preston.

I scanned the store, trying to see it from a customer's view. A common tactic Mara and I used to stage the floor, but we were also customers. I wanted to know what Natalia thought of Arcadia. It was more than a comic book store. To remain viable and profitable, Mara and I had expanded to any and every product that would sell. But the building itself was an inviting work of architecture.

The front was floor-to-ceiling windows, and skylights continued the open feel to the ceiling. Arched wooden beams mixed with metal supports to lend a trendy industrial feel to the space.

Natalia's brow formed an adorable crease when she spotted the clothing section. It was replaced by bright excitement. She beelined to the racks.

I hadn't moved. All other shoppers had filtered out, knowing it was close to closing time.

Good thing. I might growl at someone approaching the register to interrupt my spying.

Natalia flitted through the clothing racks like an evil scientist who'd found a hidden lair full of abandoned inventions. I wanted to call Mara and thank her for expanding our inventory to include pop culture clothing. Not only was it hugely profitable, but it might make Natalia a repeat customer.

She was chewing her lip over a pair of folded leggings in her hands. I couldn't tell what comic book universe they were from; I just wanted to see them on her.

Setting them back, Natalia turned and wandered to our accessories section. She passed realistic plastic broadswords and battleaxes, slowed when passing the variety of capes offered in all shapes and sizes, then stopped and smiled in front of a full-sized replica of Dr. Strange's cape.

Yeah, that was my favorite, too.

I tracked her as she moved past the costume selection to the face paint.

Face paint? Really?

She picked through an assortment and chose two. Again, I couldn't see the colors.

She lifted her gaze to scan the store.

I grinned when her eyes roved past me, then jerked back. A blush stained her cheeks.

"Can I help you find anything?" I called and started her way.

"I-I—" She looked around, noticed we were the only two now in the store, and hastily put her face paint back. "I came to ask if you can post… You know what, never mind." She flashed me an apologetic smile. "Sorry."

My strides ate the distance between us before she could run. "It's all right. What'd you come for?"

"You work Saturdays?" she blurted.

She'd only come because she thought I wouldn't be here? My earlier thrill at seeing her threatened to die a slow, painful death. Unless…she'd hoped I'd be here. Even if it were only subconsciously, I'd take it.

"Jaycee stays with her grandparents one weekend a

month. Then I work that weekend." He shrugged. "They're fun."

"Oh." Her gaze strayed to the door, but she didn't move.

I kept my tone from being too pushy or eager. "What brought you here?"

She dug in her tote and withdrew some papers. "Since you're already keeping one secret for me, we can add this to the pile. Can you hang this by the entry?"

I accepted the flyer. It was a poster for…the roller derby? "From assassin to Minneapolis Mean Streaks?"

Her flush deepened. Seeing me here had obviously thrown her, but that hadn't stopped her from sharing another part of her life with me. Was there a loophole in her fraternization policy?

Because this woman was intriguing.

So far, I'd met three sides of her, and Ms. Shaw was the oddball in the bunch. "Why the secret identity? Ms. Shaw by day, cool-as-hell chick by night?" I probably didn't phrase it the best way, but I'd never been one to hide from myself. I let my geek flag fly.

Her shoulders drooped. "I'm a principal at a prestigious private school. How seriously do you think the parents and the school board would take me if they knew I cosplayed— after someone explained what that is—and bashed into other women on roller skates?"

"Why do you care what they think?" I was no longer in the same social circles as a lot of the other parents, and my quality of life had greatly improved.

"Says the man."

Whoa. Yeah. I got what she was saying. And how could I argue? Some of the parents were nice, decent people. Others would use every angle they could to skewer someone who'd done them wrong. And if invalidating Ms. Shaw because of her social activities did the trick, they'd be ruthless.

"To be fair, being a dude who owns a comic book shop doesn't impress them either."

She smiled, then blinked. "You own Arcadia?"

"Co-own. Arcadia was Mara's idea, but when her husband shut it down, I offered to go halfsies to resurrect it."

"Her husband shut it down?"

"They weren't seeing each other then. It's quite a story. And Wes was quite an asshole then. He's not now. Not to us anyway."

"That's good." She gave the store another cursory glance. "I'm impressed with what you've done with the place. When I searched for comic book shops, I expected a closet shoved in a strip mall."

I laughed. "Like I said, Wes shut it down. Want the tour?" When she nodded, I pointed to the windows. "Wes's friend is in construction and he gave us a deal to use Arcadia as advertising. Most of what Flynn did before this was office buildings and they can only have so much flair."

"It's definitely inviting. Makes me not want to leave."

I hoped she didn't. Leading her around, I explained my and Mara's reasoning with our options and displays. Natalia nodded, her interest genuine. As long as her eyes weren't glazing, I kept talking.

The open sign had flicked off, thanks to a timer. I didn't want to be interrupted.

"This is just…" She spun around, her gaze sweeping the entire store. I'd thought my pride was boundless before her reaction. "I'm really impressed. I've never seen a comic book store quite like this. There are a couple in Seattle that are bigger than a hole in the wall, but nothing like Arcadia."

"Is that where you're from?" I couldn't help trying to get to know her.

The corner of her mouth lifted. "Sort of. I was born here when my dad was— But I call Seattle home." She gestured to the flyer I still held. "If you wouldn't mind posting that? I told them I'd drop it by, so you shouldn't have more solicitors showing up."

"Here, I'll show you where we'll hang it." She was ready to bolt and I didn't want her to leave yet. There had to be some way around the fraternization policy. Was it Preston Academy's policy or her personal one? It was a smart one, unless you actually met someone you wanted to get to know. Then it was a pain in the ass.

The bulletin board where we hung announcements was by the entrance. She was primed to leave anyway; I might as well squeak out more time with her before she jetted.

"I'll also add the information to our website. We have a community section for related events." She stopped next to me and I was about to stick a tack into it but thought better. I paused and grinned at her. "I forgot to mention there's a fee to post this."

Her eyes narrowed. "Oh yeah?"

"What's your derby name?"

Her lips twitched, reminding me how they'd felt pressed against my own. "I haven't played an official game yet." She cleared her throat and looked around, then spoke low. "Shaw Shank."

I chuckled as I stabbed the tack into the poster. "Nice. I would've thought you'd avoid Shaw. For anonymity."

She crossed her arms. "My personal and professional worlds don't normally coincide. You seem to be the exception."

My grin faded. "I wish I was *more* of an exception. Like taking you to dinner tonight."

Her arms fell and regret passed through her eyes. "Chris, I…"

The way she said my first name. So much better than Mr. Halliwell. "I know, Natalia. But I've been single for a long time and you were more than a passing interest. I don't normally kiss convention attendees."

The ridges of her cheekbones flushed. I hoped it was because she liked remembering our quick make out and not because she was ashamed of it.

"My job" was all she said, but it was half-hearted.

"Jaycee doesn't graduate for four years. I don't want to write us off because of a career." *A career that doesn't suit you.* The more I got to know her, the more I couldn't understand the Ms. Shaw side of her. Valaria? Shaw Shank? Neither of those screamed uptight principal. Neither did the form-hugging jeans that cradled her body the way I wanted to.

Skepticism entered her eyes. "I'm sure you have plenty of options."

"Have you ever tried dating—leading with 'I work in a comic book shop' and ending with 'I have a teenager'? I haven't had to lock the door against a line of single ladies waiting to ask me out."

A laugh burst from her. "Maybe if you'd quit being so hostile when someone criticizes the latest DC universe movie, you would have better luck."

"Then I wouldn't have a sexy assassin coming to my rescue."

Her laughter faded, but her smile stayed. "I think you could've handled it yourself."

"Not without losing business. They were about to diss my favorite character."

She hadn't left yet, but indecision warred in her gaze. "I just… What if we're seen together?"

I didn't want to push it and seem desperate, but I was. For her. Talking to her was as easy as talking to Mara, who'd become my best friend. But I didn't want to kiss Mara. Natalia was another story. "How about you come over? Jaycee's gone for the weekend. I don't burn too many meals since I learned to cook." If I had anything to throw together for dinner. I'd planned on having a sandwich.

"What if I have to discipline Jaycee again?" Her tone cut like Ms. Shaw. I almost sighed. Because like it or not, that's who she was.

"The first time went well. Jaycee needs to learn consequences for her behavior. My concern is her grandparents, but they're for me to deal with, not you."

She was going to turn me down. I'd have to spend the night dealing with my disappointment and bemoaning the one that got away.

"Okay."

My brows popped. "Really?" My voice damn near cracked like I was one of her nervous students.

"I won't confess my giant disappointment at learning you are a parent of one of my students, but since I don't usually lust after the other moms and dads, maybe it's worth exploring."

If her tone weren't so clinical, I'd feel better. But at least she was willing to give us a chance. "Want to follow me home?"

Natalia

NATALIA SHAW PRESTON, what the hell are you doing?

I steered my silver Lexus behind Chris's practical Ford. It was charcoal gray and not exactly what I'd expected. Since he didn't seem concerned with others' opinions, I wouldn't have been surprised if he'd rolled up with an Arcadia advertising wrap around his entire vehicle. But at the same time, his Edge fit him exactly. Understated. Efficient.

What a gorgeous store he owned. It had more artistic flair than some museums I'd been in—some art studios, for that matter. What career had he left that he could afford to build such a state-of-the-art comic book shop?

Either he or his partner had to be business savvy, and while I'd never officially met his partner, I'd gotten lost in Chris's keen gaze long enough to know he was capable.

The combo of brains and looks was why I'd embarked on this foolish endeavor to have dinner with him. Volunteering to drop off the flyers at Arcadia, knowing full well Chris might be working, was one thing. But dinner at his home? Sure, it was private, and I didn't have to worry about being seen on a date with a Preston Academy parent. But it was his *home*. It was more…intimate.

I didn't usually jump between the sheets with my dates. Usually there was a waiting period. The guy often knew my father and suspected the sum in my bank account. He'd have to show off his own talent and business acumen. When he thought I was duly impressed, then he moved in with the underwhelming physical prowess. If I orgasmed, I considered the relationship a success, no matter how short-term it was.

And they were usually brief. Even if we were physically compatible, I quickly grew stifled, holding a huge part of myself back. I wanted to see superhero movies, he wanted to see the latest critically acclaimed indie film. I'd once missed Emerald City Comic Con because my boyfriend had had March Madness fever. Was there anything more boring than a basketball game full of people I didn't know? I often attended high school games Preston Academy played in, but that was to cheer on kids I'd seen put in hours of effort—and who weren't being paid millions to play. Unless they were given a free ride to Preston Academy, which happened all too frequently. Thus, the financial issues of the last school I'd taken charge of.

I switched my concentration back to Chris. He was pulling into the driveway of a cute little clapboard house. The academy was nestled in the trees in a suburb outside of Minneapolis. Chris also lived in Eden Prairie. Should I have followed him home in my own car?

The part he lived in screamed middle-class, unlike the neighborhoods the rest of my students lived in. His house was one of many on the block; it didn't take up the whole block. I had rented a town house in a gated community in Bloomington. Maybe I should've invited him back to my place, but I didn't care to spend more time than I had to in the big, empty house.

The garage door opened, and he pulled inside. I was debating pulling into his driveway or parking along the curb when the second garage door opened.

I chewed my lower lip. We both knew we were hiding what we were doing, but parking in his garage made it sneakier. I had a job to do and someone spotting my car wouldn't help. Especially after the talk I'd had with Dresden Wentworth's parents. *Do you know how much I pay this school every year?*

Uh, probably what every other parent pays. And his separate donations shouldn't come with a list of instructions. Sometimes I wished I could say what was really on my mind. I also dreamed of drafting a disclaimer parents should sign that stated *Money donated to Preston Academy in no way makes me an authority on how it should be run. If I have ideas and opinions, I will present them at the next school board meeting. However, I will not wine, dine, or bribe my way through the school board members to sway their decision.*

I pulled into the garage with more speed than I intended,

stomping on the brakes before I went out his back wall into what was probably a tidy backyard.

The garage darkened as the door descended. I was officially on a date. With the guy who'd kept me up at night all week. I peeked at him as I gathered my purse. He was climbing out of his vehicle, the twisting motion tightening his T-shirt around his abs. How had I underplayed how good-looking he was? It was like my brain had gone into survival mode because I could plummet hard for a guy like him.

His dark blond hair rode the line between trimmed and shaggy. Intelligence shone in his eyes without the peacock displays for my benefit. His form-fitting shirt and worn jeans hugged his body at unexpected times. All of it together made him catnip to my inner puma. I wanted to pounce on him and see if he tasted as delicious as he had the first time.

He had reached my side of the car by the time I got out.

"Thanks for letting me use the garage." I glanced around. There wasn't much extra room outside of the vehicles, but he had a snowblower and a lawn mower neatly lined up on the far side. The workbench that stretched across the front was also organized, but with tools that actually looked used and not for show.

He didn't hire a lawn service. How did that exponentially increase his sexiness? I clutched my tote lest I jump into his arms before we stepped foot in his house.

"I was inventorying my kitchen on the way here," he said with a lopsided grin. Even his expressions were relaxed and unpracticed. "I've come to the conclusion that I can make you the best damn grilled cheese you've ever had, or we can order pizza."

My stomach took on a mind of its own and flipped and stretched like it was preening under the options. My nanny used to make the best grilled cheeses in the history of cheese and bread, yet I had had enough of the gourmet pizzas in the eateries I went to. Pizza was supposed to be greasy and cheesy and that quality was assumed if a place delivered.

"I…can't decide. I don't have enough of either one in my life."

"And you work around teenagers? I'm surprised." He led me to the door to the house.

"You have to remember Preston Academy teenagers aren't like the rest." Or what was the point of a private school? Our graduates went on to do spectacular things with their lives. Professionally, at least. I was living the Preston Academy dream—for my dad, at least.

His reaction wasn't what I expected. "Right? I doubt many of their dads are cooking for them each night."

I'd be surprised if their parents knew how to cook. If microwaves hadn't been invented, I would've starved. Ordering in had become so commonplace I was working on my "usual" at every place I ordered, and I'd been in Minneapolis less than two months.

Good thing I moved so often. My options changed every few years.

I stepped into his house. Even the entry was cute, with white crown molding and white trim along the walls. I dropped my purse and followed him into the kitchen. The house screamed well used, unlike the brand-new townhome I rented that was so bare not even a ghost would be interested in haunting it.

The cupboards in the kitchen were all white, but since the space was small, it worked to open it up. The cherrywood floor had to be original, but like the rest of the home, it was well maintained with a glossy sheen.

I leaned against the counter on the dining room side. There were two barstools and even though an oak table with four chairs was behind me, I suspected he and Jaycee never sat there. "I'm not as interested in whether their parents cook for them or not. I just wish the families would eat together more." Just like I'd wished my parents had been around for meals. I had enjoyed all my nannies, but it wasn't the same as feeling like Mom and Dad wanted to be around me, wanted me around for more than carrying on the empire they'd built.

"Speaking of how awesome I cook, I'm going to order a pizza." He set his phone on the counter and tapped away at the screen. "I have to admit I think there would've been more issues with Jaycee if I hadn't left my career for a more flexible job. Her mother foisting her off on me did more damage than I could've imagined."

Again, he agreed with me. I could get used to this. Usually when I brought my frustrations to the school counselor, they felt it was their duty to remind me about all the *important things* the parents were doing. I understood parents who had to work all hours to pay the bills. But working extra for the vacation home in Belize? Maybe scale back and let the kid know their parents gave a shit. But enough about work. I wanted to learn more about Chris.

"What career?" I tried to picture him doing…I couldn't come up with an example. His easy grin and Justice League T-shirt fit him so well. So did the broad shoulders and tight ass I'd glimpsed when he'd entered the house before me.

He looked up from his phone, finger hovering over the screen. "Would it surprise you that I'm a Preston graduate?"

I sucked in a breath. With that simple statement, my dream man morphed into everyone I'd ever dated before. "Seriously?" Was my dismay obvious?

"Done." He tucked his phone away. "I have an app that is too convenient. Jaycee and I have pizza night once a week, so… Anyway, Preston, yeah. That's how I met her mother. I wouldn't have been able to go, but I got a scholarship for basketball. Go Preston Knights, right?"

"What?" Now my voice was full of horror. Chris was one of the full-ride kids for a freaking sport? But—but—he was my sexy comic book geek.

"Hard to tell by looking at me, right?" He was misinterpreting my disbelief. Dammit, how could my perception of him spin on a dime? "My dad was a loan officer at a bank, and he was chatting with the president one day about my scoring average. Next thing you know, Preston was calling Dad up. My parents not being able to afford the school otherwise was foul one against me according to Cierra's parents."

I hadn't even talked to the woman on the phone. Cierra was apparently content to let Chris deal with all things Jaycee.

"Have you fouled out yet?" I asked, surprised I could match basketball lingo with Chris.

He grinned and my heart stopped. Those shoulders. His height. I pictured his strong body going in for a jump shot, his focus on the hoop. I didn't usually go soft over athletes, but when they had a fanboy personality, it was a potent combination.

"Yes, which brings us back to your earlier question about what I'd been doing for a living. Before I got full custody of Jaycee, I was on the city council for Minneapolis. That wasn't prestigious enough to impress Cierra's parents, but I had just gotten elected to the state senate. I stepped down before I even started. I couldn't be away from Jaycee for those long days."

I blinked. He was a *politician*? An athlete and a politician? And a Preston grad? I apparently wasn't straying from the type I'd sworn I wouldn't date again.

His smile died. "That bad?"

I tugged one of the stools over even though I shouldn't be settling in to stay. "It's not that." I owed him more of an explanation since I must've looked horrified. "I mean, yes, it is. I've dated guys just like you and it hasn't turned out well. But I guess I've never met any of them at a comic con."

"That's the key."

A smile tugged at my lips. "Is it. Does it go the other way? Have you dated other women like me?"

"That's a resounding no. They've all been disturbingly similar to Cierra." He went to the stool next to me and we faced each other like we were at a real bar and not in an old but well-cared-for house. "You've heard similar stories. Guy tries to marry girl. Girl's family thinks he's trash. Breakup and serial dating of the exact same type occurs."

"You wanted to marry her?" How old had he been?

"The sun rose and set with her—at the time. But she made her opinions known." His expression darkened like he was remembering the pain it had caused. "My dad worked for the bank president instead of *being* the president. And my mom sold insurance; she didn't own the company. All those fouls against me and they thought it was better to have an unwed mother for a daughter."

"Ouch." In this day and age, that shouldn't be a scandal, but it would be for the families who attended Preston.

He lifted a shoulder, only bringing attention to how close he was and how much I liked gripping his shoulders. "It worked out. We're both grateful we didn't marry, and now she's happily dating and reclaiming those lost years when she was stuck with a child at home."

"Role reversal?" This probably wasn't the sexiest topic but learning about him had become my new favorite pastime.

"You could say that." He lifted the hood on my sweater and dropped it. "Looks like I'm not the only Preston Academy grad in the room."

"Ding, ding, ding." The last thing I wanted to talk about was the school. Dresden still hadn't served his detention and if he didn't show after school on Monday, the battle went to round two. "I went to the one in Seattle." And Hartford, Atlanta, and Chicago.

"Was it as stuffy and uptight as this one? No offense." He winked.

"They try to be." I gave my voice the same inflection as Alfred the butler. "We have standards to maintain, Master Wayne." I sighed. "It's exhausting."

"Being the villain is never easy."

"At least they seem to be having fun in the comics." Or believed in what they did. "Every bad guy is the hero in their own story. I guess we'll have to see whether I'll prevail or not."

hris

"You're right," Natalia announced. "It's better the second time around."

I had known she'd agree. I shut the TV off in the middle of the rolling credits and massaged her feet as she reclined against the armrest of the sofa. We'd had our pizza. I hadn't asked her preference when I'd ordered, but I hadn't wanted to interrupt our conversation. And the way her eyes lit up when I'd mentioned it, I'd pegged her for a cheese or Canadian bacon girl. Or pepperoni, but I couldn't stand the stuff, not even for a hot fangirl who looked adorable in my living room.

That was a lie. I'd eat all the pepperoni if she demanded it. Especially if she was in that tight bun and skirt when she did it.

Digging into the ball of her right foot, I enjoyed the way her eyes glazed over. "I'm kind of disappointed you've only seen *Suicide Squad* once before tonight."

She leaned her head on the armrest and closed her eyes. "Didn't I mention that I prefer Marvel movies?"

I ran my finger up the bottom of her foot. She squealed and jerked her foot back. I followed, stretching out on top of her. "You take that back."

Her sharp inhale and the desire that flared in her eyes encouraged me not to back away. She stared up at me, her eyes luminous, her body molten underneath me. That damn sweatshirt was covering the best of her curves. It was no longer as cute as it had been in the store.

"I guess we're done watching movies?" Her breathy tone ignited the lust that had been simmering all evening. She shifted, her legs parting to cradle me.

I settled farther over her, propping my arms behind her back to spare her from an awkward angle. Our mouths were a whisper apart, but I didn't close the distance yet. "Is there anything else you want to see?"

"I came here to see you and I happen to be exactly where I want to be." She pulled her lower lip between her teeth. Had she surprised herself? Because I was delighted.

Dropping my head, our lips touched. I took my time, savoring the satin of her lips, the way her chest pressed into me when she took a breath. She opened for me first, her tongue darting out.

Yes. I'd been dreaming about her body for a week, but it had felt like months. A low rumble reverberated in my chest as I deepened the kiss. She tasted like the sparkling strawberry water we'd been drinking—fresh, fruity, and tingly.

She skimmed her hands up my back and my shirt bunched up with the effort. I'd take it off, but I didn't want to break the kiss. If it were up to me, I wouldn't break the kiss all night. Her embrace tightened as she surged into me, rubbing her pelvis against mine. I'd been half hard around her all night, but blood rushed to my groin until my erection was painful and aching. I answered by rocking into her.

To keep her from being crunched into the corner of the sofa, I maneuvered one arm between us to tunnel underneath her sweater. Her skin was soft, hot, and so smooth I didn't think I'd ever be able to keep my hands to myself around her. The inviting curves of her back ran under my hand until the lace of her bra hit my fingertips. Deftly tucking my fingers under the band, I tested its resistance. The elastic gave easily until I could lift the bra above her breasts.

I closed my hand over a warm mound of flesh, and she arched into me. It was hard to maintain the kiss with an arm between us and our frantic undulating. I abandoned her mouth to nibble a path under her chin. She shivered in my arms, her moan echoing in my ears while her legs wrapped around my hips.

I wanted her naked, but it was too soon. Having her in my house, in my arms, was more than enough. She was willing to risk discovery, but if we took it too fast, too soon, she might talk herself out of exploring how strong this connection was between us.

I trailed a path with my mouth to her collarbone, my face tucked into her sweatshirt. Rolling her nipple between my fingers, I debated lifting her top to get at it with my lips, but she was straining under me like she wanted more, needed more. I abandoned her breast, my hand mourning the loss of her heat, and found the waistband to her pants.

I almost cheered when I realized it was an elastic waist, no button or zipper. Weren't those called jeggings or something? I didn't care at the moment. For once the state of women's fashion didn't perplex me. She'd loosened the hold her legs had around me, creating enough of a gap I could wedge a hand between her clothing and skin.

Blood hammered through my cock. Losing the stimulation of her rocking against me was maddening, but it was just as satisfying seeing to her pleasure. I got my own pleasure from her breathy gasps and the way she writhed against me.

The material of her underwear was lacy like her bra. I bet they matched. Ms. Shaw didn't go for unmatched undergarments. Maybe someday I'd get to see, but tonight I was content to ride the wave of sensations between us.

I dipped under her panties. Her skin was hot and the farther I went, the wetter she got. Her excitement made it easier to slide a finger through her folds.

She jerked in my arms. "Chris." I was about to quit when she went liquid and rocked her hips up into me. The move stroked my finger along her clit and she moaned.

Emboldened, I circled her nub again and was rewarded with another breathy moan. Those sounds were going to haunt me each night I went to bed alone. I'd never be able to go to sleep with a cold shower and stroking one off again. I'd been deluding myself for years that I wasn't missing this.

And I wasn't really. I wasn't losing out on anything with the wrong person. I was missing this with the right person.

She fit me perfectly.

I changed positions to rub her clit with my thumb and thread a finger inside of her. She was wet and tight and so hot I didn't need any stimulation to worry about coming in my pants. Her hips thrust against me, seeking a release. She groaned and moaned, giving me a glimpse into the uninhibited woman who could dress like Valaria and play a contact sport like roller derby. How many saw this side of her?

I was selfish to hope I was the only one.

"Chris," she whined again. Oh yes. A guy could get used to a woman begging for her release in bed. I'd never felt more powerful. Not after I won the election, not after Arcadia's opening day, not in any other intimate moment. No other woman made me feel like I should don a cape and stand proudly with my hands on my hips.

I wanted to kiss her again but muffling those erotic noises would be a sin. Instead, I licked and nibbled along her neck as I circled and thrust with my hand.

Her legs had untangled from around my waist until they were drawn to her sides.

My forearm threatened to cramp, but I adjusted my position.

"Don't stop," she barked. At some point, she'd wound her hands through my hair, pinning my head into the crook of her neck.

Heat flooded my hand and she tensed. "Chris!" She bucked and cried out.

My hair got pulled as she jerked and shuddered, but I could only smile. I was in a state of pain with the throb of my erection, but I was a happy man.

She stilled and her grip eased. I lifted my head, unable to hide my huge grin. I kept my hand where it was, still inside of her but no longer stimulating the bundle of nerves.

"You look proud." She sounded accusatory, but the smile playing along her lips ruined the effect.

"I kinda am. That was pretty spectacular." I slipped my hand out. Desire flashed in her eyes. I couldn't bring myself to withdraw from her clothing entirely. She was everything warm and feminine I'd been dreaming about in a woman, someone who didn't laugh off my interests and hobbies as juvenile.

"For me, yes. You did all the work." She placed her hands on my shoulders and was starting to push me back, a predatory gleam in her eyes, when the Batman theme song from the sixties burst through the room.

Crap. Jaycee was calling. I couldn't exactly ignore it.

Natalia reclined back, leaving me half sitting up. "I'm guessing only the really special people in your life get that ring tone?"

I chuckled and grabbed my phone off the table. My heart sank when I saw the screen. Collapsing into the opposite corner of the couch, I met Natalia's gaze. "She wants to FaceTime."

A flash of panic passed through Natalia's eyes. She pushed into a sitting position on the opposite end of the couch. Once she gave me a nod, I answered and Jaycee's green goop-covered face filled the screen. No wonder she didn't just call. She didn't want to get her phone dirty, and she liked to try to shock me. This kind of startle I didn't mind.

"Hey, kiddo. What's up?"

It wasn't unusual for Jaycee to call on the weekends she was gone. Her grandparents alternated between smothering her and neglecting her. And there was always the lunch with Cierra. I never knew how that'd sit with my daughter.

I shifted into a more comfortable position. Once I'd seen my daughter's name, all lust had vacated the premises.

"Nothing. Nana has friends over. Some stupid work thing. Papa's helping her out." Nana and Papa had an aversion to the "grand" part of parenting. Nana had insisted Jaycee call her that since before she could talk. So to be devilish, Chris had always called them that, too.

"Boring AF?" I used her father-approved substitute for *as fuck*.

Jaycee smiled, lines forming in her face mud. "Boring AF." She always got a kick out of me using her terminology. She'd deemed me "not that ancient" at the ripe old age of thirty-two.

She leaned closer to the screen. "What's up with your hair?'

"Uh…" I used my free hand to brush it down. My gaze

strayed to Natalia. She was pale, like she was slowly dying inside. Damn, I hoped this phone call didn't ruin things between us. "I was lying on the couch watching a movie when you called." Not a complete lie.

"Wild, Dad. I can't even with your Saturday nights."

I met Natalia's wary brown gaze and looked back at the phone. "I was doing exactly what I wanted to. How was your day? How's your mother?"

My whole personal situation would be shittier if Cierra and I didn't get along as well as we did. We weren't buddies, but we didn't hate each other. The first few years had been hard, and I couldn't blame Cierra for being snippy while going to college and raising a kid. I'd been too hurt by her complete rejection. I'd been an okay rebellion, but she wasn't going to get stuck with me for life. Her parents had nearly abandoned her but had been afraid it'd make them look bad. I'd done everything short of marrying her to help. She appreciated it now, somewhat. At the time, it had been a different story.

"Mom's Mom." Jaycee's typical answer. She looked to the side and her frown cracked the goop. "She's engaged."

"What?" That was a surprise. Jaycee hadn't mentioned her mother was seeing anyone. Neither had Nana and Papa.

"Yeah. I wasn't the only one shocked." She jerked her head toward where the door must be. I didn't spend a lot of time at her grandparents' house.

"Nana didn't know?"

"Nope." Jaycee shoved a hand through her hair and folded the hand she held the phone with around her knees. Natalia had grabbed her own phone and was scrolling through it to give me a sense of privacy. We were both too afraid for her to move and make noise that'd clue Jaycee in that I wasn't alone.

"What do you think?" I asked.

"Well, I haven't met him." Her tone was heavy with disappointment and betrayal. "I asked if she was going to have more kids."

I tensed. "What'd she say?"

Jaycee ran her tongue in front of her teeth. Her mask was cracking further from her facial movements. "Probably, but"—Jaycee made air quotes with her free hand— "'not in the near future.'"

When she was grown and out of the picture, was that what she thought? And how hard would it be for her to watch the mother who'd dumped her on my doorstep have other kids and live happily ever after?

"Having kids in your thirties is different than at eighteen." Cierra and I hadn't been much older than Jaycee when Cierra had gotten pregnant. My stomach soured. That time had gone by fast.

"Right?" Jaycee gazed away from the screen, her expression sullen. "It's not me, it's her?"

"Basically. But it doesn't feel like it, huh?"

Her eyes glistened, but she blinked it away. "Just in case she was thinking about having bouncing babies of joy, I told her I got detention this week."

I stiffened. *Please don't say anything about Ms. Shaw.* The same Ms. Shaw who'd just orgasmed in my arms. I recovered and gave her a stern look. "Did you tell her it was over a boy?"

"No, I told her it was over a feminist principal with something to prove. Maybe Nana needs to donate more so I can get out of detention like Dresden."

I should've been mortified, but I was triumphant over finally learning the other kid's name. "Dresden Wentworth?"

Could Jaycee have hooked up with a wealthier family? The Wentworths had adamantly opposed my run for state senate. Dresden's dad had been a few years older than me, but he'd taken the bench on the basketball team when I had shown up.

When I chanced a look at Natalia, she'd lowered her phone and her eyes were narrowed on mine. Had Dresden really gotten out of detention, or did Natalia not want him and Jaycee to know?

"Busted," Jaycee said. "I know you don't care for his dad."

"I don't give a crap about his dad, and he's not a fan of mine." It had been a good thing that Cierra's baby belly hadn't shown until after graduation, or the Wentworths would have caught wind of the scandal and gunned for me to lose my scholarship. Then I would've had less time and money to offer Cierra than I'd had.

An alarm went off. I looked around, but it was coming from Jaycee's end.

"Gotta rinse, Dad. See ya tomorrow?"

"Are you coming to the store?" She used to love Arcadia. But in the last year, she'd shunned all things in the geekdom.

"I'll probably just have them drop me off at home." She palpated her face, squinting into the screen. I'd lost her to the face mask.

"Call me when you get home. Love you, kiddo."

She disconnected and I tossed my phone to the table.

"How much did you hear?" I joked.

Natalia's cheeks had lost their post-orgasm flush. I wanted to put it back, but she was in Ms. Shaw mode. "I can't argue. I *am* a feminist principal with something to prove."

I chuckled and dropped my head back. "Couldn't she have picked someone besides Frederick Wentworth's son?"

"It would've made life easier for both of us." Natalia sat forward on the couch. I hated to see her leave. My real concern was whether she'd want to see me again. "And no, he didn't get out of detention. You and his dad have a history?"

"Remember that scholarship? I showed up sophomore

year, and what should have been his year to shine was not. He rode the plank as a senior while I played." We'd titled that year.

"That's too bad."

Something about her tone was off. I'd heard it before, from other students and their parents. "Too bad that he wasn't a better player than me, or too bad I got the scholarship that made it an issue in the first place?"

She pursed her lips, then rose. "I should go."

"Natalia…" Should I apologize? As if judgment throughout high school hadn't been enough, I was still getting it from the principal. Only she was my date.

Natalia straightened her clothing and crossed to the bar, where she'd left her shoes before we'd eaten on the couch. She shoved her feet into them and grabbed her tote.

"Are you going to talk to me? What's going on?" I couldn't escape the feeling that if she left with only a goodbye, I'd never see her other personalities beyond Ms. Shaw.

"Jaycee's call was a reminder of why I shouldn't be dating parents." She pushed her hair off her face and finally looked at me. "This really can't happen again."

"I want it to."

Her gaze jerked away. "Me, too. But it can't. I've worked too hard to get where I am and to get taken seriously as the founder's— Well, my career and the school's future is riding on my efforts. I can't wipe them all out when someone sees me with you."

Natalia skirted around the bar to cruise through the kitchen. She paused at the picture on the fridge. Hadn't she seen it before? It was a colored pencil sketch of Pegasus that Jaycee had drawn in blues and purples with a silver overlay. Her work was all over the house.

"The artist is Jaycee," I explained. "We joke that the house is her gallery. I used to rotate them, she worked so fast, but in the last year…" It was the same story with her behavior. I'd been saying "in the last year" a lot.

"It's stunning." Natalia continued to the back door. "I just can't risk my work at the school."

"I understand. But at the same time, I don't envision the Ms. Shaw I met being a woman who's pushed around by the other parents and their ignorant opinions."

Natalia's shoulders stiffened. Her step faltered before she was back on track and beelining out the door. "Good night, Chris."

"Have a fun practice tomorrow."

Climbing into her car, she paused and looked up at me.

"The poster," I explained. "You have roller derby practice Sunday afternoons."

Only the corner of her mouth lifted, but the crease between her eyebrows didn't promise another date. She got into her car and I hit the button to raise the door. She drove away, leaving our time on the couch behind us both.

I had to see her again.

What would it take to find myself in the principal's office once more?

atalia

COULD someone get more professionally belligerent? As Frederick Wentworth droned on about his various contributions to the programs at Preston Academy, I let my mind drift. What was it like to work for him? Did his wife get her way or was he a tyrant at home, too? They had to have Dresden as a young couple, but I was sure Frederick finished his schooling while his wife probably had to drop out and raise Dresden.

Dresden showed promise. He was walking in his daddy's footsteps, but in a blink, I saw the kid underneath who wanted to shine for his own reasons, not the ones ordered by his father. But Dresden was a junior and by next year, the assimilation would be complete.

Sometimes those cases were the hardest. How did I balance a kid's best interests versus their parents' wishes? How did I determine which was which?

Either way, Dresden risked his position on the football team with one more failing grade. He'd grudgingly, and with great dramatics from his mother, served his detention. They'd stretched it into two after-school periods for maximum punishment for me.

I wasn't one to turn to drink after a hard day, but between those two evenings, I'd killed a bottle and a half of merlot. And I hated wine.

I couldn't wait until roller derby practice Sunday. The release of aggression couldn't be beat.

Uncrossing my legs, I switched ears. Why hadn't I used my headset? Frederick Wentworth liked his own voice too much to keep the calls short. A message from Ms. Branson flashed on the computer screen.

Jaycee Halliwell is in the office again.

It was unusual for Ms. Branson to remain cryptic. I tuned back into the man spewing words on the other end of the line. Frederick had made it up to last year's donations. Did he have an eidetic memory or was he keeping a running tab of all the checks he'd written to the school? Maybe he'd gotten the amounts tattooed on his wife's ass so he could get a good look at them every other night.

Natalia Shaw, behave. Threading the no-nonsense steel back into my spine hadn't been easy since that night with Chris. His words about not letting myself be pushed around still rang in my head. They should give me more gumption, decrease my level of fucks to give, or increase the swagger I strutted around the academy with.

Nope. I only played a ruthless assassin, and not even on TV.

It was like those words had had the opposite effect. I had slunk into my office and slammed the door behind me, startling Ms. Branson, if the rattle of the woman's coffee cup was any indication. After my own high school experience,

Priscilla Wentworth's snide and sometimes outright hostile comments after detention shouldn't have affected me so badly. Yet I had driven home with my hands shaking on the wheel.

Dresden's mom was exactly like the girls I'd gone to school with who never let me forget for one millisecond that I got favorable treatment only because I was the owner's daughter.

Want on the cheer squad? You were so bad, not even your daddy could help you.

I had begged my mother not to intervene.

Ooh, look, you got first in debate. How much did that cost your daddy?

As if my father had even known I was on the debate team.

Aw, that's horrible. Who threaded a tube through your locker slats and drained an entire liter of sports drink into your locker?

Who exactly?

People just like Frederick and Priscilla Wentworth.

Memories of my epically shitty school experience hadn't bothered me for years. Why in Minnesota?

Because I had more to hide here. Not just being the granddaughter of Godfried Preston, the mighty founder of Preston Academy, but...Chris. Because all I wanted to do was don my mask and keep seeing him.

But the number one reason I couldn't was waiting outside my office. I didn't bother messaging Ms. Branson back. My assistant must think the issue didn't need an explanation.

Students came first and that gave me enough titanium grit to cut off the speaker on the other end of the line. I rolled out my typical speech when dollar amounts were thrown in my face. "Mr. Wentworth, on behalf of Preston Academy, I can't thank you enough for your generosity. As you know, the forms you sign when enrolling your child at the academy state that any and all contributions will be used to better the school and will be allocated at the discretion of the school board. As always, your child's preparation for the future is our greatest responsibility. If you have any concerns, please check the website for the next school board meeting."

"Ms. Shaw—"

"I'm terribly sorry, but there is a student here to see me. Send all further inquiries to the school board. Thank you for your time, Mr. Wentworth." I hung up. The school board had hired me for this very reason. It had been a contentious decision, but the bottom line spoke louder than the dissenters. They wanted me to be their tool of change and save the school from financial ruin.

Some of them didn't know I was a Preston, either, which was a bonus. My history of molding academies back into shape had spoken for itself.

I went to the door, using the opportunity to stretch my legs. Mr. Wentworth had kept me anchored to my desk for too long. Peeking my head out, my stomach sank to the rock bottom of my sensible pumps.

Jaycee hadn't noticed the open door yet and her head was turned as she stared mutinously out the main office window to the hallway. Her electric-blue hair had been neatly curled and hung over one shoulder. Fuchsia streaks topped the look and made Jaycee a beacon in the room. All the administrative assistants were purposely not looking at Jaycee or in my direction.

I sucked in a fortifying breath. Ms. Branson glanced up from her computer screen. The gravity in her expression said enough. It didn't matter how cute Jaycee's new 'do was, it was against Preston Academy's dress code to artificially color hair. Everyone knew it and it was oddly one of the rules that I had never had students butt up against. Most kids didn't want to go through the effort and expense of dying hair only to be ordered to return it to its normal state. The effect on the health of the hair was enough for children who'd grown up self-conscious about blending and achieving a standard.

After Jaycee's round of detention and counseling, she knew full well that something as drastic as blue hair would propel her to the next level of discipline.

Suspension.

Fuck it all, I didn't want to deal with this today. I'd wanted nothing more than to hear Chris's voice, but not like this.

And I didn't want this for Jaycee. Knowing the personal issues and self-doubt and low self-esteem the girl was dealing with, I didn't want a setback like this for the girl. The mother who'd given the girl up was getting remarried and had mentioned starting a family.

That had to be the motivation behind the blue hair.

At the same time, I could throttle the girl. Did Jaycee know how hard her dad worked for her? How much he'd given up to spend quality time with her?

Time to be the bad guy. "Jaycee. Come in, please."

The flare of anxiety in Jaycee's gaze disappeared immediately. Rebellious obstinance was there to stay.

I stepped aside and shut the door once Jaycee stalked past me. Jaycee wore khaki pants today with an emerald shirt. Was her choice deliberate? The color of green clashed outrageously with her cotton-candy-blue hair.

Once we were settled in our seats like the first time, I gave the girl a hard stare. "Why'd you do it?"

"It's just hair dye."

"What'd your dad say?" Had Chris sent her to school, knowing this was going to happen? Didn't he know he could call with concerns?

Another reason why going home with him had negatively

impacted my work. I couldn't let my personal desires interfere again.

"He didn't even notice," Jaycee said bitterly.

I raised a brow. "Blue hair isn't easy to overlook. You hid it from him."

A flash of guilt. Jaycee was an emotional girl trying to appear like an immovable mountain. "I wore a hat. It's cold out."

"And you know that unnatural hair colors are against Preston Academy's dress code."

"The color blue is found in the wild."

"You're not a macaw."

Jaycee's lips twitched. Seeing the humor in the situation wasn't a bad thing, but Jaycee hadn't taken the effects of her actions into consideration. Her hair session had been all about Jaycee and no one else.

"You're going to be suspended for three days." I fortified myself against Jaycee's reaction.

"Cool." Not even a hint of regret resonated in Jaycee's voice.

"Don't you want to go to school here?"

The answer rippled over Jaycee's youthful features. She didn't want to go to school here, and she barely covered her relief at the suspension.

"Why not?" I leaned over my desk.

She didn't answer. Her lips were pursed, her arms crossed in front of her chest. But her hair was cute. If I didn't have to worry about a dress code, I could chuck my itchy wigs and experiment with colors for cosplay.

"Jaycee, you just started high school. Thanksgiving break will be here in a few weeks, then Christmas break shortly after that. Take each school year by chunks. I promise that graduating will be worth it."

"Ooh, I'll have a diploma that says I can follow the rules

and nothing else. I can apply to college and show I can get passing grades but have no athletic talent whatsoever. They'll be lining up to let me in."

The girl's tone should irk me, but the message underneath was too important. "What about your drawing?"

Jaycee frowned. "How'd you know about my art?"

My chest constricted. My mind flashed to being wrapped in Chris's arms. How was I going to explain this?

"It's my job to know things about students." That was the biggest pile of crap I'd ever shoveled. Would Jaycee buy it?

"Lot of good it does me." Jaycee's gaze slid out the window, where the gray overcast sky should be the same color blue as the girl's hair. "Do you know that there is not one single art class available? But we have to take phys ed— for both semesters each year. And play flag football," she finished bitterly.

I sat back and assessed her. It wasn't often that a kid wasn't a good fit for the school. Brains and brawn were treasured more at Preston Academy than artistic skills, and parents tended to raise their kids in their image. Ceramics wouldn't conquer Wall Street.

And even if I wanted to add alternative programming with the argument that it molded well-rounded students? There wasn't the money. Offering ten full-ride scholarships to football players, another five to basketball players, and three more for track stars cut into the budget. All the teachers were paid more than in public schools, with the sought-after health insurance and retirement perks to go with it. It was critical to retaining excellent staff.

But it wasn't the scholarships sinking the school. Investing in the students wasn't where my concerns were. It was the expectations placed on the large donations from alumni and current families. I had to plan for the drop in contributions when I dropped Thor's hammer on the spending funneled into the sports programs.

Arguing that touchdowns didn't conquer Wall Street was as welcome as the Death Star was to Alderon.

Was Jaycee the only student feeling the pressure, or just the only one fearless enough to say it? Punishing her and telling her to suck it up seemed counterintuitive to helping her grow into adulthood.

"Tell you what." My mind reeled through possibilities and my own excitement increased. What would Jaycee think? "While you're suspended for the next three days, research what other schools do for their art programs. Types of classes, a club versus a course, and if you're ambitious, the cost of each option."

Jaycee's mouth set in a troubled line. "That sounds like a lot of work for it to end up just another stack of paper on your desk."

I scanned my desktop. The wide computer screen and keyboard were set to the side and five ordered piles of paper filled the rest.

I tapped a finger on the closest pile. "Health insurance plans." I moved to a new pile with each description. "Performance evals. Continuing ed options for the staff. School year calendars for each school in the district. And everyone's favorite, pay sheets."

"I thought you were like, a teacher or something."

"In many schools, the principal is a teacher, not that they do much teaching when they reach the office. Preston Academy is a bit different. I'm still a trained educator, but my function is more administrative."

Her gaze landed on the papers. "You'll really consider it?"

"The school board has the final approval. I can't promise anything." I hesitated with my next thought, but it wouldn't be fair to falsely raise her hopes. "I'll be honest. It'll be a hard sell. That field isn't a priority to the families that send their kids here. But coming armed with data is the first step."

"All right. I'll do it. If only to show the school board that this place is lame."

"Sometimes the motivation isn't as important as the outcome."

Jaycee raised a skeptical eyebrow. "Getting deep there, Shaw—Ms. Shaw."

"Nice save." I sought out the phone on my desk like it was a phaser set to kill. "Why don't you wait out in the main office while I call your dad."

I waited until Jaycee walked out before dialing so the girl didn't notice that I knew his number by heart.

hris

I LOCKED UP THE STORE. My Saturday to work, and I'd spent the whole day waiting for Natalia to wander in like she had a month ago.

Jaycee was with her grandparents. Neither one of us had told Nana and Papa about her suspension. My elation at hearing Natalia's voice on the other end of the line that day had crashed like Kal-El's spaceship.

But Jaycee had thrived under the punishment, spending each day on the phone to various schools.

Dad, did you know that studies show art education can improve students' entire high school performance?

Look at this place. The whole school is built around the arts. Dance, drama, visual arts.

I wonder if a summer program would work for Preston.

I hadn't seen my daughter this fired up since Cierra had enrolled her in a summer art program. Jaycee had loved every minute while my heart had broken. Cierra had only put Jaycee in that place so she wouldn't have to deal with her daughter.

I was wandering back to the register to cash out and do end-of-shift paperwork when my gaze caught on the Minneapolis Mean Streaks flyer. I'd looked up their website —and every social media site they could possibly create. For reasons.

Their season hadn't started yet, but they did clinics and recruiting workshops.

A date snagged my attention. Tonight, they were having a special holiday scrimmage against the St. Paul Pinup Punchers as a fund-raiser.

How stalkerish would it be to show up there? It's not like I had anything else going on.

I thought about it while wrapping up my paperwork and storing the cash in the safe. It wasn't like Natalia had to know I was there. And I was insatiably curious to see how Shaw Shank dressed for roller battle.

Once I closed the store, I trotted to my vehicle and climbed in. Glancing down at my jeans and red T-shirt with a lightning bolt, I shrugged. Pretty sure I'd blend.

I was across town within minutes, the traffic sparse this time of night, and Arcadia wasn't far from the community center.

More cars lined the lot than I'd expected. I searched for Natalia's. What if she wasn't here? At least I'd have some-thing new to tell Jaycee.

So wild, Dad.

The aged brick building looked like two square boxes shoved together. One was smaller and probably housed offices. People were filing into the other one through two white double doors.

Young girls disappeared inside dressed like Jaycee usually

did when she wasn't in her school uniform, their shoes brighter than the rest of their subdued outfits. And their hair was colored like Jaycee's had been the day Natalia had called me. One girl's was short, purple, and shaved on one side. Another girl's hair was pitch black and spiky.

Would Natalia have suspended Jaycee over pitch black? It was a natural color.

I tried not to be bitter. Some of Preston Academy's rules were outdated, but they hadn't been changed—yet.

Just like their course curriculum. Outdated. Created when all things male and athletic were thought to be the determining factors for success.

I wandered through the doors and stopped to pay the attendant with a black star painted over her eye and a two-tone ponytail. I handed her a twenty. She smacked her gum and gave me a smile that would've given me pause if I were here for anyone other than an uptight rule-follower-slash-assassin.

She gave me a ten-dollar bill back. "The children's hospital thanks you for your donation." Cocking her head, her gaze landed on my shirt. "The Flash, huh? We like fast guys here."

I chuckled and walked away. The more she talked, the younger she seemed. She was probably still in her twenties, but the gap between us could just as well be decades.

And I wasn't fast when it counted.

People milled around the corridor outside the arena. The buttery smell of popcorn filled the air, and next to the last entrance into the gym was a stand full of souvenirs. The game wasn't supposed to start for fifteen minutes and it wasn't going to be a full house. I went to the table. Christmas tree ornaments of gold and silver roller skates hung from a three-foot tree. A couple skates had the Mean Streaks' logo painted on them. I marveled over the crafting.

The rest of the table was littered with eye patches in a variety of shapes and colors, crazy hair ties that would get Jaycee expelled from school, and face-paint kits—also with the derby team logos.

I bought a few scrunchies for Jaycee's Christmas stocking, and to show Mara for ideas of what to bring into the store. Arcadia could carry items like these from local events and use it as a promotional gimmick. Win-win for both parties.

There. I was thinking about work. Now I didn't feel like a creeper hunting down a woman who'd told me we shouldn't see each other.

I entered the gym. Music thumped from a pair of speakers anchored on the opposite wall. The lights were dim, but the rink set up in the center was under spotlights. The bleachers on either side were half filled. Add in the people outside the gym and it was a respectable turnout.

I scanned for the skaters, but only a few young women were working the crowd, handing out pamphlets and inter-acting with the kids. A video screen in the middle played clips from previous games. I chose a seat on the end of a row in case Natalia spotted me and looked horrified.

My phone buzzed with a text from Jaycee. *Nana's not feeling good.*

I replied, *Papa, too?*

Out for the night. Mom picked me up and brought me back for supper.

How'd it go?

U know. It's Mom.

As long as Jaycee kept communication open, I wouldn't worry. She was talking about it even if she wasn't diving down deep into her feelings. Except she hadn't mentioned Dresden since they'd both gotten detention. Was she seri-ously interested in the kid?

God, I hoped not. It didn't matter what Dresden was like.

His parents were the issue. I didn't want Jaycee to repeat my history.

My phone vibrated again. *Supposed to snow tomorrow night.*

She must be really bored. *I heard.*

She didn't text back, and I was staring at my screen when the lights blinked off. The family next to me broke into applause.

The rumble of several pairs of skates on hardwood echoed through the bleachers. The lights flicked on. One of the women who had been roaming the crowd was now in the middle of the rink with a microphone.

Applause broke out around me and I joined in. My heartbeat kicked up a notch.

Where was Natalia?

The first team introduced was the visiting team, the Pinup Punchers. I clapped and laughed with the crowd at the players' names. The whole team had their hair tucked and curled like pinup models, and they all wore a combo of yellow-and-black tops and skirts, all with the same 1940s calendar-girl style. But their face paint made them unique. Some had bloodred or black lips, others had black lines under their eyes like football players, and others had yellow eye shadow. Their elbow- and kneepads were black, but their shin socks were striped with both colors. Yet none of them came off as looking like a bumblebee.

Introductions over, they smashed their black-and-yellow helmets on their heads and skated to the side. The age range surprised me—some as young as the attendant to women that were older than me.

"All right, all you nice people," the announcer hollered. "Time to introduce you to the Mean Streaks!"

I clapped with the crowd, but I was searching for one woman only. As their names were called off, each skater broke away from the pack in a dim corner on the other end of the gym and skated a lap around the track.

The Mean Streaks wore black fitted tank tops and leggings or tights—some fishnet. Most skaters had streaks of color painted up and down their arms and across their faces. The helmets were black with the same slashes of color and their safety pads were red.

Five names were called before Shaw Shank.

Natalia skated out and I wanted to run to the side of the rink for a closer look. Her team cheered and whistled. The look on her face was all Ms. Shaw.

But her body was all Valaria. Toned legs were hidden by webbed tights that weren't exactly fishnet but were a lacy pattern that summoned the memory of her on my couch. Her tank top was fitted and the muscles that filled out her Valaria costume were on display.

If I hadn't known her skating name, I might've recognized her on sex appeal alone. But her hair was braided, her eyes were rimmed with black makeup, and her lips were sexpot red. She also sported a purple-and-yellow smear of color on each cheek.

I grinned the first ten minutes of the game. Natalia wasn't as experienced of a skater as some on her team, but she was fearless, her face a mask of determination. Each time she skated by during her jam, her mouth was set in a hard line, her lips were rounded out from her mouth guard, and her eyes flashed with intent. I had to search *roller derby rules* on my phone to understand what was going on. She was a blocker, trying to keep the jammer from scoring by passing opposing team members.

My smile faded when Natalia was knocked down by a Pinup Puncher, Lauren PenaltyCall. Natalia hit her knees but popped back up. The aggressiveness of the sport wasn't lost on me, but it was different when it was someone I cared about.

How many players broke bones?

The rest of the game I white-knuckled through, cheering when others around me did. The player that butted Natalia out of bounds had continued to target her.

Shaw Shank was going to be sore in the morning.

Relaxing when Natalia sat out a jam, I glanced at the time clock. The game was almost over. Would I be able to track down Natalia when she was done?

Would she want me to?

In the final jam, Natalia was back in play. So was Lauren PenaltyCall. I sat forward, my hands fisted in my lap. The intent was clear in Lauren PenaltyCall's narrowed eyes. They made one lap around, the breeze from their passing blowing across my face. The section closest to the rink, the suicide section, cheered each time the skaters raced past.

I eyed the clock. Two more minutes left. Natalia had already deflected an elbow and zipped around a skate meant to trip her. Where was a ref when you needed one?

My heart pounded. The teams were neck and neck. Had my parents felt this way? I'd caught an elbow to the face in a couple of basketball games, but it was nothing like this. Jaycee didn't play sports and I hadn't gone to any games since I'd quit playing in college.

The jammer for the Pinup Punchers was darting around Natalia when Lauren PenaltyCall moved in to block her. Only the woman's skates tangled with another player's and she flailed to the floor. Natalia tried to jump over her, but Lauren PenaltyCall was still rolling. I rose, already jumping down the stands, when Natalia hit the floor, the crack of her helmet echoing across the gym.

Collective gasps rang through my bones and the lights were flipped on.

Women were already at Natalia's side, the group so thick I couldn't push between them.

"She all right?" I called, but no one paid me heed.

The group backed off, pushing me farther away. Musky sweat mingling with perfume surrounded me as I tried to shove my way past.

Curious glances were thrown my way, but I ignored them until I made it to Natalia's side. I dropped to my knees next to a man and woman, both wearing a white shirt and navy-blue medic pants. EMTs.

Natalia was flat on her back, blinking at the woman. "Yes, I remember my name. Let me back in the game."

I couldn't hear the woman's reply, but Natalia waved her off and surged to a sitting position. She scrunched her face up and rubbed her neck. "Oof. That hit was harder than I thought."

"You really should get checked out," the male EMT said, but Natalia shrugged.

"I had my helmet." She knocked lightly on the headgear and winced. She unhooked the chin strap and took the helmet off. Her gaze landed on me and she frowned. "What are you doing here?"

I was about to answer when the EMT interjected with more questions. I didn't leave her side as they moved her farther away from the rink since she stalwartly refused medical care.

A woman who must be in charge of the Mean Streaks skated up after murmuring with the female medic. Her helmet read Thriller Killer. "Do you at least have someone to hang out with you for a while?"

Natalia's gaze strayed to me and I quirked a brow. When she didn't dismiss me, I dipped my head.

"Yes," she grumbled. As she slowly skated the perimeter of the gym, the crowd cheered. She grinned and waved, but she couldn't hide the tension in her face from me. She was hurting.

Thriller Killer faced me, her bright blue eyes serious. "Can you pull up to the door? I'll walk her out after we get her things. And try to talk some sense into her."

"Good luck. Is there a door by the locker rooms that's closer?" I got directions and jogged out to my vehicle.

The night wasn't ending how I'd planned, but if I hadn't come, who would she have had to help?

Natalia

I LEANED my head against the headrest of Chris's car and suppressed a groan.

It wasn't the dull throb of my brain getting rattled, but the rest of me. Too bad Thriller Killer had only given me an ice pack for my head.

"I wasn't knocked out." I sounded whiny, but I was allowed to. I was sweaty and my paint was streaking. My tights hadn't had a long life expectancy, but they were toast after that fall. A huge rip went from my knee to under my shorts.

"You've mentioned that a time or three." Chris's deep voice was a verbal massage my entire body felt. It'd been a month since we'd seen each other and three weeks since I'd last talked to him on the phone. I'd counted every day.

What was he doing at the game?

Oh. Jaycee was with her grandparents.

I snuck a peek at him out of the corner of my eye. It was worth the twinge in my temples to see his profile. Borderline shaggy hair spilled over his forehead and his lips were in a stern line. The concentration he aimed at the road sent my nerves stumbling over each other. The face he gave the rest of the world was congenial, aloof at times. Always easygoing. But he could be intense and focused at the best of times.

This wasn't the best of times and he was still hot.

He glanced at me. "How are you feeling?"

"No different than the last time you asked." I shifted the ice pack off my head and set it on my shoulder.

"That player had it out for you."

"Yep. I'd swear she was bought off by one of the students, but no one knows I play."

He flashed a smile at my joke. "Is her thing to go after the noobs?"

I nodded, pleased that my head didn't start pounding.

"What would you have done if I wasn't there?"

Wasn't that the question of the day? As if I hadn't been panicking about facing the medical gauntlet on my own until I realized I could refuse treatment.

"I don't know," I whispered.

"Why are you so secretive, Natalia? I don't get it. I mean, I get your job. But with your whole life?"

"How do you know I'm secretive outside of work?"

"Do your parents know about cosplay and derby? Ms. Branson?"

"Ms. Branson's an employee, so no. And no, my parents don't know." My mom's reaction would be ten times worse than when I had joined the Star Trek club as a senior. I had meant to stick it out, but when the car had gotten taken away and my bank account suspended, I'd submitted.

Clubs based on fiction are useless in our nonfictional world.

Thanks, Dad. It was one of my first lessons in keeping my private life top secret. I needed to be taken seriously for the stellar work I did, not the hobbies I enjoyed.

Chris's house came into view. A welcome sight. I'd

prepped for a long night of ice and acetaminophen in my empty townhouse, but Chris's home was so much more…homey.

I'd rather not talk about my nonexistent social life. "Have you lived here long?"

"I cashed in a savings account when Jaycee started living with me full time. The place I had before…" He shook his head. "Pretentious condo in the heart of yuppie city. I don't think one other child lived on the whole block."

Well, didn't that describe my place?

"My parents moved to Arizona ten years ago," he said. "Cierra's apartment at the time was as big as a phone booth. Cierra's parents live in a mansion that Jaycee can't paint, color, or get rowdy in, so I thought a traditional home would be better for her."

"It's nice."

He chuckled as he pulled into the garage. "Nice. I guess that's all I can ask for."

"It's more." He parked and the garage door shut behind us, but I didn't make a move to get out. "My place is…expensive. Trendy. Contemporary. The only reason I look forward to going home is because my king-sized, deluxe-pillow-top bed is there. And my TV. It takes up half a wall."

"Well, let's get you inside before you remember my TV gets lost in the wall." He got out and I did the same. "Do you need fresh ice?" he asked as he retrieved my gym bag from the back seat, leaving my bag of gear behind. My tendency to overpack had worked in my favor for once. It was my first scrimmage, and I hadn't had many practices. My Valaria costume might be fitted from neck to ankles, but my jam shorts were…short. And my tights managed to show more than they covered. If I hadn't worn so much padding, I would've been blushing down to my knees, and cosplay assassins shouldn't blush.

"This baggie is still good, but I could use another pack."

Chris unlocked the door and held it for me. "Go on in and get comfortable. I'll make us something to eat."

I slowly picked my away across the garage. My muscles had stiffened on the ride but were loosening with each step. A bruise on my right side where Lauren PenaltyCall's elbow had clipped me was aching. It probably felt worse than it looked, but that could be said about my overall appearance.

"Thanks," I muttered when I stepped into the house. I meant it. Between my headache and my body aches and feeling like an epic failure for getting taken down by an over-bearing brute, my inner Valaria wasn't even prepared to open an energy bar. "Mind if I use your shower?"

"Knock yourself out." He smiled when I quirked a brow at him. My heart fluttered with that damn twinkle in his chestnut eyes. "Not literally. Why don't you use mine? Jaycee's is the first door on the right upstairs, but she's not a regular cleaner and there's no counter space left. But I have a small bath off the master bedroom at the end of the hall."

"Thanks again." I trudged for the stairs, not needing directions. We hadn't made it off the couch last time I was here, but his house was compact.

Rounding a corner, I stopped. The landing for the stairs was as ordinary as the rest of the house, but the artwork on the walls captivated me. Pain pushed aside, I drifted around the perimeter of the small square, its area the size of a jail cell. Scratch art. Was that what it was called? The private schools and boarding schools I'd attended weren't heavy in the arts. But it had to be. A solid black background overlaid a colorful palette of reds, whites, and oranges. On another, there were various shades of green, and a third was blues and purples. The hues were unveiled by delicate and deliberate scratches.

The effect itself was stunning, but the panorama of the

three smaller pictures together was the most impressive. Intricate leaf patterns were revealed in the greens. Flowers and petals in the blues and purples, and sunset in the oranges.

They had to be Jaycee's creations. The girl had talent.

I flipped the light on and ascended the stairs. Now that I'd been moving a good few minutes, I wasn't as sore and welcomed a shower.

But I stopped at the landing.

"Holy artwork, Batman." More scratch art, an obvious favorite of Jaycee's, but on the second level the drawings were straight from graphic art. Across from me was scratch art in shades of gray, with silver predominant. An artistic risk that worked beautifully because the girl had outlined Batman from the side. He was running and his cape billowed behind him.

Another was in blues and reds, with a scratched outline of Captain America's shield.

My lips quirked at the third. Another orange palette—with Sonic the Hedgehog.

What if I gave Jaycee a blank scratch art canvas with deep reds? Could she do a full-body profile of Valaria? One of me walking like a badass toward, or even away from, the camera?

Shaking my head, I ripped my gaze away and scurried down the hall. I couldn't slip up around Jaycee again. A kid who had served detention and been suspended wasn't going to be keen on keeping my secrets.

Avoiding peeking into Jaycee's room was a struggle. I wasn't a snooper, but Jaycee's bedroom probably rivaled an art gallery, only way more relatable than the ones I had been to in the past. My dates had been as boring as the artwork. Jaycee's work was definitely up my alley.

If Jaycee and I had been teens together, she would've been

the girl my parents forbid me from ever talking to. Fan art equaled useless trash in their minds.

I slowed when I got to Chris's room. It wasn't because of his—oh my god, was that a Dark Knight pillowcase? I crossed to it. His bedding could put *Fifty Shades of Gray* to shame; it was contemporary with clean lines. The sheets, though, were an ode to Batman.

That shouldn't make him sexier, but it did. Who'd he date that would be turned off by a grown man with superhero bedding?

I shook my head and scanned the rest of the room, my ponderings swerving to concern for Jaycee. My gaze touched on a full hamper, a matching walnut dresser set that must've been from his white-collar career-man days, and closed closet doors. Was Jaycee facing the same attitude from her peers as that of my parents? *Not good enough for my kid.*

I'd have to keep an eye on Jaycee. Many high schoolers were outgrowing the overt bullying of younger kids, but they could be insidious, or worse, not realize how hurtful they were in their comments around others. Too self-absorbed, they'd had empathy trained right out of them. But some were mean just to be mean.

Taking my bag into the bathroom, I dropped it on the tiled floor and rummaged through my protective pads, makeup bag, and spare pair of tights. I had the sweats I'd worn to the community center but no fresh underclothes.

My sweaty sports bra had dried. Uck. I didn't want to put that back on after I showered. Same with my underwear.

How obvious would it be to go without? I was a generous B cup, but my sweatshirt was fluffy. Good enough.

It's not like I would cozy up to Chris close enough for him to find out I wore no underclothes.

atalia

REFRESHED after my shower and free lady-balling it, I went downstairs. The savory smell of grilled bread and butter hit my nose. My mouth watered. I'd been living off grilled chicken and salad greens all week. They were fast and easy; all I had to do was buy each separate and dump them together with the right seasoning. But that didn't stop me from occasionally wishing there was something deep fried to accompany my meal.

"Is that grilled cheese I smell?" I called, making my way to the kitchen. Two plates were on the bar. Each held a couple sandwiches cut in diagonals, just like a restaurant would do —or my nanny. Next to the sandwich were strawberries half the size of my fist and sugar snap peas.

"Holy carbs, Batman, this looks delicious." I slid onto a stool. A can of sparkling lime water was waiting by my spot, along with a bottle of acetaminophen. He was either that sweet, or his dad-ness was showing, or both.

"I figured if you were open to grilled cheese last time, it must be a safe option. And I don't often find good strawberries this time of year."

He sat next to me and we both carved through the meal. By the time I was done, I couldn't keep my eyes open. It was almost eleven and I'd had a long day.

Chris must've noticed my heavy sigh and long blinks. "Go ahead and take my bed for the night. I'll sleep on the couch."

Part of me was disappointed that I was at Chris's and I was going to eat and go to bed. Okay, all of me was disappointed. But I had to be responsible above all.

I was standing when he said, "Don't be creeped out if I come up to make sure you're still breathing."

"I don't have a concussion." I didn't think I did. Wouldn't I feel worse?

"Medic's orders." His gaze dipped to my chest and tore away. No bra. Right.

My cheeks warmed as I put my dishes by the sink. "Good night, Chris."

"Night. Holler if you need anything."

I went back upstairs, pausing only briefly this time to admire Jaycee's work. In his room, I crawled between his sheets and was encompassed by his scent. Fabric softener and shea-butter Suave shampoo. His aftershave was one of my favorite smells, but he must shower before bed. Was he going to use Jaycee's bathroom?

I drifted to sleep. Hours later I woke. What time was it? The hallway light was left on and the bedroom door open. I peered at the clock on the nightstand. Two thirty in the morning. Enough time for my ibuprofen to wear off, and the acetaminophen I'd taken with supper was flagging.

Swinging my feet down, I waited for the pounding in my head to swell, but it stayed at a dull throb. The pain was only a four on a scale of ten, but it was enough to keep my achy body from falling back asleep.

I made my way downstairs, wincing each time a stair creaked. The old house's groans weren't as noticeable when people were up and moving around. In the middle of the night, I might as well shout "I'm awake and coming down."

A groggy and blinking Chris rounded the corner by the landing. His hair was disheveled. My hand twitched to run through the silky strands. He wore the same lightning bolt T-shirt but had changed into black basketball shorts. I half expected a Bat-Signal somewhere on the fabric, but he wasn't as overtly fanboy as many others. I liked the subtlety of his interests.

"Hey, what can I get you?" His sleep-roughened voice was deeper. Instead of being tired and wanting to go back to bed, I wanted to hear him talk more.

"I just wanted some acetaminophen and maybe a glass of OJ if you have it. I didn't mean to wake you."

He started for the kitchen. "I'll grab it and bring it up."

I watched his broad back as he puttered through the kitchen. Giving myself a mental shake, I turned and went back upstairs. The bed was still warm, almost too warm with my sweats. I stayed sitting up but left the covers off.

He appeared down the hall and headed my way, a glass in each hand. The flutter in my stomach was undeniable. My own superhero in basketball shorts. He had nice legs. The muscles in his quads and calves bunched and flexed with each step. Basketball does a body good.

Did he still play, or had he traded the ball and hoop for comics and capes?

Playing probably didn't hold a place in his life while

running a business and raising a kid. Yet he'd gotten a full ride at Preston. What good did that do him? Had he gone to the same college he would've gone to without his Preston Academy pedigree? Had he gotten a full ride for all four years because of his time at Preston?

He approached the bed and held out the glass of juice. "How was the sleep?" He dropped a pill bottle on my lap that he'd been holding with his glass and drained his drink.

"Good." I downed half of mine before getting two capsules out. "Thanks." A word I'd been saying around him a lot. I swallowed my pills and polished off the cold drink.

He lifted my glass out of my hand and set it on the nightstand with his. I froze when he reached over me to grab the covers. "What are you doing?" With him so close, memories from our evening together bombarded me and my body said to hell with the aches and pains. The pleasure he could bring me was much more desirable.

He frowned. "Just tucking you back in. Don't you want the covers over you?" Drawing away like he'd finally noticed his proximity, he released his handful of comforter, but I curled my hands into his shirt.

"I don't know if I can go back to sleep." Really? That was the best I could say when I was preventing him from backing away? Not that he was putting up any resistance.

"Doesn't your head hurt?" His voice had dropped low, and even with his face shadowed from the hallway light behind him, his gaze simmered with barely restrained heat.

Pulling him closer, I whispered, "Not if I'm properly distracted." When had I sounded so needy?

His lips landed on mine and I continued tugging him toward me as I lay back. He kept his weight on his hands and knees as he captured my mouth.

We both groaned into the kiss. It'd been too long since

the last time we'd been together. His weight was a welcome burden and I wore the anti-Valaria equivalent of clothing—baggy sweats.

He kissed me slowly, as if he were waiting for me to shove him off at any moment. But I wouldn't. Unless he objected, I had no plans to back out. It had been a shitty workweek of arguing with righteous parents and their entitled children, followed by slogging home to an empty house, topped off by getting strong-armed off the track during what was supposed to be an entertaining, lighthearted scrimmage.

No, the real topping was staring at the asbestos-filled ceiling of the community center, squinting at the low-hanging lights, and wondering how the hell I was going to manage if I had a concussion, an injury that required someone looking out for me.

Enter Chris. He'd come to my game. It was his weekend without Jaycee, and he'd been thinking about me, too.

I broke from his scorching lips to whisper, "Take my shirt off."

He rocked his hips forward, the hard length of him barely restrained by the flimsy shorts. His gaze drilled into me like he was assessing my ability to make such a decision. The blow to my head hadn't knocked the desire out of me. But resolve must've been obvious in my eyes because he sat back on his knees and rolled the hem of my sweatshirt up.

I lifted enough to get the sweatshirt over my head. His breath whooshed out as he dropped the garment on the floor.

The way his gaze raked my torso… I might have to make another cosplay character. Valaria's twin sister Salaria: sexual goddess.

With my legs splayed on either side of him while he perched on his knees, I had nothing else to do with my hands but relax them behind my head.

"I thought you were sexy as hell the first time I met you. I think I like you best with no clothes on."

I wiggled my hips. "I still have my sweats on."

He gave my breasts one last lingering look before hooking his fingers into my waistband. A brief thought of whether I should take a more active role crossed my mind. But the way he handled me, so carefully, like I was fragile, was too intoxicating. I liked being taken care of, even if it was for a fling.

Was that what this was?

I brushed the question off. Too much thinking about the future. Always on guard, always planning my life around what others thought. In this bedroom, it was just us and the sizzling chemistry we had.

A draft wafted over my belly as he tugged my pants down. Deftly moving off the bed, he slid them off.

Another breath puffed out of him as his gaze swept from my breasts to my bare sex down to my toes. "You weren't wearing any underwear? I might've choked on my grilled cheese if I'd known that."

I smiled. "Are you saying you would've gone out of your mind with lust while I was wearing a thick coat of cotton armor?"

"You make those sweats looks sexy. Don't ever doubt that."

I cocked my head. His sincerity floored me. My clothing had been warm and functional. Nothing like the athletic wear that showed as much as my Valaria outfit, which I enjoyed wearing, too.

He hadn't moved since he dropped my pants. Self-consciousness was setting in.

I caught his gaze. The heat in his eyes stole my breath. He ripped his shirt off and dropped his shorts.

It was my turn to gasp. I rose on an elbow. The words

"You work out" left my mouth before I could consider how inane they sounded.

The corner of his mouth kicked up. "I do."

His broad shoulders were one of his best features—when he was dressed. But he had a tight body carved from a lifetime of taking care of himself. He might feed me pizza and grilled cheese, but he didn't subsist on greasy food alone.

And his manhood. Thick and straining, it was as hard and defined as the rest of him. This geek was hiding an Easter egg under his clothing—*Surprise! I'm really a jock.*

I tracked every flex of muscle as he bent to the nightstand and withdrew a box.

Condoms.

My mind screamed *Yes!* but I bit my lip. He pulled out a foil packet and was setting the box back when he frowned. Straightening, he turned toward the hallway light and squinted at the box.

His shoulders slumped. "They expired last spring. Like, nine months ago."

"What?" I sat up, but that put me at eye level with his erection. Actually, that wasn't a bad place to be.

"Shit." He tossed the box and the packet to the nightstand. "I'm sorry."

I giggled. Only two responsible adults would fret over the expiration date minutes before they were going to insert the hard cartridge into the needy game station. "Not to ruin the mood, but I'm trying to think of anyone under the age of twenty who'd be deterred by an expiration date."

His mouth quirked. "That's how I had Jaycee."

"Well, I'm on birth control if that's the main concern."

"I've obviously been abstinent for a while."

"Then…" I shrugged. "Let's use them."

His gaze stroked my body. He leaned over and grabbed a condom, ripped it open, and rolled it on.

My belly fluttered with nerves as he crawled back on top of me. But I didn't have time to dwell as he lowered his head and captured my mouth.

He was sweet, like the juice we'd had. I twined my arms around his neck and hugged him close. We weren't separating for anything. No other foreplay was needed beyond seeing him naked.

I cradled him between my thighs and rolled my hips into him. Sensing my need, he positioned himself without breaking the kiss. The pressure of his broad head promised he'd fill me like I'd never experienced before.

I surged up, taking him inside. He tensed, like he was afraid to hurt me. But he felt too good to slow down now. Digging my hands into his ass, I pulled him toward me.

Letting out a gasp, I arched into him enough to rub my aching breasts against his bare chest. He set a hard pace. There was no playing around, no *does this feel good, how about this*. He took what I offered. We strained against each other, nipping earlobes, nibbling lips, and it was exactly what I needed. Heavy breathing intermingled with moans filled the air.

Stretching out the pleasure should be my goal, but nothing but hormones and want drove me. Tightening around him, I dug my nails into his back and cried out, my climax slamming home.

He stiffened above me, his thrusts shortening as he let go. We came together and for a few moments, it was just us. A couple. No history between us or behind us.

Languidly kissing me, he withdrew. Curling up with him was the only goal on my list for the night. The endorphins chased away aches and pains and my meds would kick in soon. He left only to disappear into the bathroom. By the time he came out, my lids were too heavy to keep open. But I hoped he stayed.

The bed dipped with his weight before I was wrapped in his warm embrace. It was just the two of us. For now, this would have to be our little secret. My small smile lasted until I fell asleep.

CHAPTER 9

Natalia

LIGHT PEEKED in from behind the blinds, casting slatted shadows across the wall and bed. I extracted myself from Chris's side, where I'd been planted since we'd fallen into an exhausted sleep.

My body aches had returned and not the just the delicious stiffness from the sex. I glanced at the nightstand where the expired condom wrapper lay by my empty juice glass. No bottle of pain meds. Damn. I'd have to get out of the warm nest to get some.

But there was a slumbering naked man to come back to, so…

I scooted to the edge of the bed and swung my legs down. The covers fell off and air wafted over my bare body, sending shivers across my skin.

Sliding off, I dropped to the floor to snag my sweatshirt. Wait. It wouldn't cover my ass, but Chris's shirt would fall to close to my knees. Then I didn't have to waste the energy to step into my bottoms.

With his shirt, and surrounded by even more of his scent, I tiptoed downstairs to keep from waking Chris.

A muffled rumbling sound was coming from the living room. I crept to the entry. His phone was vibrating on the end table. I'd bring it up to him when I got the water and meds.

Turning back to the kitchen, I spotted the acetaminophen bottle on the counter. Perfect.

I dug out a capsule and found a glass to fill with water. Tossing back the pain reliever and gulping down the water, I was turning when voices grabbed my attention.

Frowning, I looked around. The main window was in the living room, and thanks to my state of undress, I didn't want to creep out there any farther than I had to for phone retrieval.

It was Sunday and…I sought out the oven to peek at the time. Whoa. It was almost eleven. I'd wonder how I slept that late, but I'd been up in the middle of the night. And busy.

An engine sounded like it was passing by. A faint door slam made me jump and spin around. The water in my stomach swelled like an alien was going to burst out.

Rushed footsteps and the creak of the garage door opening pushed me back into the counter.

My usual mantra of *What Would Valaria Do* didn't come to mind. Not even my fictional wannabe inner tough girl could help me out of this nightmare.

Jaycee rounded the corner. "Dad! I've been trying to call —" She stopped so fast her shoes skidded on the hardwood. "Ms. Shaw?"

Jaycee's gaze swept from my bedhead down to my bare little toes. My breath choked to a standstill in my throat. I couldn't speak. I wanted to scream. I'd rather an alien bust out of me and spare me the career-ending mistake I'd just been caught with.

"*Ms. Shaw.*" Scandal dripped from Jaycee's tone. "You and my dad?" An overnight bag I hadn't noticed dropped from the girl's hand.

In my mortification, I couldn't help but think that Jaycee's look fit her so much better than the stuffy uniform dress code of the academy. Skinny jeans, an oversized maroon sweater—the letters *MCU* probably slid under her grandparents' radar—and a pair of high-top black Vans. Her hair was twisted in a side ponytail that draped over her shoulder. She looked refreshingly fourteen and comfortable in her own skin, unlike her usual demeanor at the school.

I gulped. "Jaycee—"

A light brow arched. "What happened to Ms. Halliwell? Is that just in the walls of Preston, or once you hit it with a parent we're on a first-name basis?"

No, that was Mr. Budinsky.

"Jaycee," Chris snapped. His welcome, yet completely unwelcome heat surrounded me as he sidled next to me. He was wearing the shorts he'd had on earlier and had found a dark shirt. My attention was too absorbed by the unfolding drama to note what was on it. "Why don't you head to your room for a couple of minutes while Ms. Shaw—Natalia and I —talk."

"*Natalia*, is it?" Jaycee crossed her arms and kicked a hip out. "Why? You two want to get your story straight? Nope."

I cringed. All my principal bluster had vacated. I was in someone's house, in a situation I'd sworn I'd never put myself in, and I couldn't fall back on my professional ways. I had no idea how to act. Put me in a boardroom and I ruled the meeting. Slip into Valaria's costume and I kissed strangers in public. Mingle with the sponsors at faculty parties who didn't care to talk to me anyway and I could make an excuse to leave early.

But deal with a date's kid? Foreign territory.

Deal with a kid outside of "Preston's walls"? What the hell should I say?

"Natalia needs to get dressed," Chris spoke evenly. "Please give her a few minutes of privacy."

"Nuh-uh. I want to hear the story. How long have you two been hooking up?" Jaycee's gasp was indignant. "Dad, did you let your girlfriend suspend me?"

"Jaycee…" Chris rubbed the bridge of his nose.

"Who else knows? Oh my god. Was it my tardiness that was the love connection? How—"

My last nerve snapped. "Jaycee, your father asked you to wait in your room." I sucked in a breath. That wasn't called for, but dammit—I wasn't wearing a bra or underwear!

Jaycee reared back, her gaze seeking her dad's.

"Please, Jaycee." Chris's weariness soaked his tone. Great. Was he upset at me now?

Jaycee hitched up her bag and wandered past them. "Call me when the warden allows me out." Her footsteps pounded up the stairs and her door slammed shut.

"That could've gone better," Chris muttered.

"That shouldn't have gone at all." I massaged my temples. My current headache had nothing to do with my fall the previous night, and my body aches had been forgotten as soon as Jaycee had entered the premises. "I should've been gone hours ago."

"She doesn't usually come back this early, but she said Nana wasn't feeling well. With the snow coming, I doubt they wanted to risk having Jaycee an extra night."

They sounded lovely. I stuffed my sarcastic thought away. I would be happy to leave Chris and Jaycee to it. But I needed to be in on "the talk."

"Why don't you go get dressed?" Chris's gaze strayed to where Jaycee had disappeared up the stairs. "I'll make us all something and we can talk over food." My look must've been dubious, but the corner of his mouth lifted. "It'll bring a sense of normalcy to an otherwise awkward discussion."

Yeah. As if any of us had an appetite. With a sigh, I headed up the stairs, grateful Jaycee's door was shut. I'd done enough of the walk of shame without moving an inch in the kitchen. And there'd be no fleeing once we finished discussing what Jaycee had walked in on. My car was parked at the community center. I'd either need a ride or have to call for one.

I dressed, sucking up the unwashed sports bra and putting it on, and grabbed my bag. Facing the door to the hall, my stomach roiled. I wanted to vomit and run and run while vomiting. Was this what kids felt when they were sent to my office?

Natalia

DOWNSTAIRS, I slumped on the stool I'd used before, but after a sidelong look from Chris, I moved over. That must be Jaycee's spot. Chris finished boiling some spaghetti and warming up meatballs and sauce. It was the lowest-maintenance pasta dish I'd ever seen made. And I probably couldn't make it by myself.

Jaycee probably could.

I sunk my head into my hand. "What do you think she'll say?"

"I don't know." He frowned as he stirred the sauce. So far, he'd cooked me two meals and ordered out one. If we were to keep seeing each other—not that we should—I should treat him to a dinner. Takeout or dine out. My cosplay alter ego should've been a sous chef. Maybe then I'd have learned to cook.

Funny how my parents had fretted so much over my future, but they hadn't ever taught me one basic survival skill —how to cook. Neither one knew how. They'd always had a personal chef. But they could've ensured I knew the basics, just in case.

I had been taught to sew by a favorite nanny, Beth—a fact that would have made Mom die a slow death, punishing me for it every minute, if she'd ever learned it. Other kids hid their alcohol and cigarettes. I'd hidden my Singer in the back of my walk-in closet. But my pattern-reading ability wasn't helping me here.

I fiddled with the hem of my top. "Can I get the plates and stuff?"

He gestured to the cupboards to his right. I evaluated his expression as I skirted around him to get plates and silverware. His mouth was a flat line and his dark eyes grim. Was he worried about his daughter, or me? Or both?

"I'm really sorry," I murmured. I set the items on the bar but didn't sort them.

Without a word, Chris pulled the pot off the stove and dumped the water and noodles into a strainer. He set the pot on a pad and sighed. "I don't need an apology, Natalia. I have a beautiful woman in my home who I like talking to and have a great time with." He glanced at me, heat flaring in his eyes. Yeah. We had a great time. In and out of bed. "I'd love for my daughter to know about you. Is it just your job?"

It wasn't just a job. It was my career, the one I'd been groomed for. And I was excellent at it, thank you very much. If the price of respect was strict adherence to the school's policies to keep my parents from interfering and the school board from questioning each and every change I implemented, then yeah, it was my "job."

I chose another way to explain. "I have to fight for every ounce of respect. From the staff, the parents, and to some extent the board. It was a contentious decision to bring me in, but it was me or see the school fail. And I have a proven track record."

He nodded but didn't look at me as he puttered around, getting serving bowls for the food. "I get it. I don't like it, but really, the decision is yours."

To keep seeing each other. It'd always been up to me and I was tired of having to resist.

He studied me, but when I didn't reply, he went to the base of the stairs. "Jace, come on down."

Jaycee's entry was quieter than her departure. Chris had been right to let her cool off. I met her steady stare.

"You two ready to explain yourselves?" Jaycee slid onto a barstool, but her ghost of a smile was promising. Unless she was just really happy to see spaghetti.

Chris took the seat between us. We should've chosen the table, but I doubted father or daughter ever thought of sitting there. The table was for show.

As we each took turns dishing our food, Chris explained. "I met Natalia at TCCC, before I knew she was your principal. Afterward, we weren't going to see each other, but she came through the store to drop off a roller derby flyer and we got to talking. Then last night I went to her game, she got injured, and I brought her here to care for her."

Jaycee twirled her fork against her plate. "Is that what the kids are calling it these days?" She leaned across the bar to squint at me. We really should've sat at the table. "Is that why you came down on me so hard?"

I wasn't sure if my answer would make things better or worse. If I wanted to keep seeing Chris, if I wanted Jaycee to keep my relations with her dad under wraps, I had to be transparent. "No, that's how I normally am. I don't sugar-coat my job. That's why the school board hired me. I get them back on track with the school's policies, up to standard."

I shoved a forkful into my mouth. Simple carbs, easy to digest. Just what I needed this morning. Both because of the exercise and because my stomach was as tight as my customary hairdo at work.

Jaycee frowned at her plate. "I thought they hired you because your father owns the schools."

I coughed around my mouthful and reached for a napkin.

Chris set his fork down. When my coughing died down, he asked in a measured tone, "Is that true?"

Wiping my mouth and catching my breath, I cursed the loose lips that had led the gossip train to Jaycee's door. Was it any wonder that Valaria and her world of secrets were appealing? By the time Valaria took out her hit, she was gone. She didn't get caught with no underwear in the kitchen.

"My grandfather founded the academy. My father took over after he passed away. My original last name was Preston, but I had it legally changed after college." The truth spilled out and maybe I should've hidden my vulnerability, but I'd never been able to talk to anyone about the name change. My parents hadn't understood. "After going through high school with the last name Preston, I didn't believe being 'Ms. Preston' would win me any credibility at work. It's hard enough being a woman in the traditionally male-dominated world of Preston Academy."

Jaycee snorted. "I would've thought that it'd give you a free pass. Not like belonging to the scandalous teen mom with a dad who's more likely to wear a cape than a suit to work." She elbowed her dad to take the bite out of her words.

I saw the move for what it was. Jaycee would rather have

a dad in a cape than work a job for prestige and appearance's sake.

We were making progress. I explained further. "My interests and hobbies weren't like the other kids, and my parents kept trying to steer me in the 'right direction.'" I gave the last two words air quotes. "But I was raised by nannies and their interests became my interests. Blockbuster movies. Graphic novels. Anime. Mother was livid when she learned my first nanny had so atrociously influenced me." I smiled. "But the next nanny had kids. Blissfully normal kids, and I lived vicariously through her stories of them."

"Sounds familiar." Jaycee stabbed a meatball. "Only instead of a nanny, I have Dad."

Chris chuckled. "I figured that was the reason you don't hang with me at the store like you used to."

"Are you kidding?" Jaycee rolled her eyes. "It's not like I'm the ugly duckling at that place. It's like the rest of the students are the swans and I'm the duck."

Chris rubbed her back. "You out-swan them. And it's only for high school. Nana and Papa don't get a say on where you go to college."

"You'd better have my back." She offered him her knuckles and he fist-bumped her.

I had to look away. I would've traded in my private driver, my summers abroad, and my trust fund to have a relationship like these two had.

Jaycee tipped forward to peer at me again. "So, Ms. Shaw? Roller derby?"

"Even big girls like to do things that'd make their parents apoplectic. And it's a great way to relieve stress in a way where the two worlds I exist in don't normally collide." I snuck a peek at Chris.

"But Dad tracked you down?" Jaycee giggled. "Stalkerish much, Dad?"

He nodded. "It occurred to me you'd say that."

Jaycee waved her fork toward us. "Now what? You guys going to keep seeing each other? Am I going to have to be all secret agent and pretend you're not dating my dad?"

I exchanged a glance with Chris. "I'd like to keep dating." I'd like to actually *date*. "But if I did, we have to keep it out of the academy. And if you come to school with purple hair, I can't look the other way, no matter how cute it is."

Jaycee's eyes widened. "You liked the blue?"

"If I didn't have to adult on a daily basis, I would chop my hair and play with colors." I may have sketched out a few headshots of the funky styles I'd love to try.

"Dude, the principal thing is a total fun suck. Fine. I can play the game. It's not like anyone talks to me anyway. Dresden's moved on to cheerleader chasing." Jaycee leaned in and whispered, "I don't think they make it much of a chase."

I grinned. At least Jaycee seemed to have moved on and wasn't nursing heartbreak. "As long as it's not on school grounds, then I don't have to deal with it."

Jaycee barked out a laugh. I turned my smile back to my plate. A girl could get used to this. Fun banter about a serious topic over a meal with people I enjoyed being around.

As long as Chris was on board, I'd take it slow. We'd date, keep it on the down low, and when my work at Preston Academy was done, I'd have to move.

hris

I closed the store and refrained from sprinting to my vehicle and not because the temp had dipped below zero. It was the first Saturday that my daughter was back at her grandparents' since Jaycee had busted me and Natalia. While Natalia and I had continued seeing each other, it'd only included movies at my place while she and Jaycee ranked Marvel heroes.

Natalia had practice, and between her job and my store, Friday-night dinners and Saturday movies were the only times we could get together.

But I was done for the weekend and Natalia had invited me to her place.

I followed her directions, which brought me to a tall, wrought-iron gate. Pulling up to a speaker box, I entered the code she'd given me. The gate buzzed and swung open.

This wasn't the ritziest gated community in the area, but I

didn't doubt she could afford to live where she chose. This place had townhouses and that was probably the reason there wasn't an armed guard out front. Proper rich folk lived in proper mansions, and a townhouse failed in that measure. I tried to adjust my mindset. This could've been my world. I'd been on my way. My state senator pay on top of the private consulting job I'd been head-hunted for would've left me with an enviable salary, a nice pension, and enough to buy a three-story brick house with a pool house in the back-yard that I could even use in the frigid Minnesota winters.

I might've filled in the pool and had a basketball court constructed, much to Jaycee's dismay. Not that I'd been plan-ning it at all…

Did I regret giving my old life up? Jaycee was well-adjusted. Her mom was happier. I liked my coworkers better. The kids we hired for the shorter shifts usually accepted my mentoring and I'd been in the job long enough to see them finish college and move on to careers of their own. I liked thinking that I'd helped build some of those skills they carried forward with.

If Jaycee weren't at her grandparents' mercy for school-ing, she would probably work at the store, too. I rubbed my eyes.

Cierra's parents. They'd started asking Jaycee about what she planned for college. Against my advice, or because I'd advised her not to, she planned to present them with the art program data she'd compiled for Natalia, which included colleges with fine arts programs and the different tracks available.

I fully expected their disapproving frowns on my doorstep when they dropped her off tomorrow.

Just one more reason to spend the night in Natalia's arms.

I pulled into the drive. The garage door opened and wow, what an empty space. She didn't even have a shovel. Definitely no snowblower; this wasn't the neighborhood for it. They all hired lawn services and Natalia liked to blend.

My forehead crinkled. I understood the way she'd grown up didn't inspire deviation from the norm, or what her parents considered above the norm. Despite being a woman in her thirties, she didn't seem comfortable living life on her own terms.

The garage door shut me in, and Natalia appeared at the door. Her leggings and oversized Captain America shirt were as sexy as they were adorable.

"Hey." Her grin widened when I pulled my overnight bag out of the back. "I ordered in supper. I hope you don't mind. I don't cook."

Had she worried I'd expect something fancy? I slung the bag over my shoulder and strode toward her. "We could've gone out."

Panic flashed in her eyes. "No. I like eating in." She smiled. "With you."

Yeah, but eating out with me? I brushed off my worries. We were dating, as much as we could be, but she continued seeing me despite her regimented ideals. For now, I'd be happy with what time I got with her.

She was about to spin to go inside, but I twirled her back to me to land a kiss on her plump mouth. She melted into me, and I didn't care if the savory smells of fine dining wafted out of her place, I needed to feel her.

We hadn't done more than kiss in weeks, both of us too timid with Jaycee under the roof.

She moaned and wrapped her arms around my neck. Our tongues twined and memories of our night together surfaced. Her straining against me, her pleas, and the tight fist of her sex.

I was hard and throbbing in an instant. But really, the buildup had been a month in the making.

I broke away enough to pant, "I don't want to wait until after dinner." Then I lifted her.

Her legs circled my waist and I twisted to press her against the wall by the door. Could she be feeling the same urgency?

"Then don't."

I paused. Had I heard her right?

"Dinner will wait," she said in husky tones that went straight to my erection.

"Just a quickie to take the edge off?" I rocked against her. So close, but so much between us.

She released me to work at the clasp of my pants. "I've been dying to be with you again."

I anchored her with my hips and dug in my back pocket. "I even grabbed fresh condoms." That box of expired condoms had almost prevented the best sex of my life.

"Me, too." She inhaled when she freed me, circling her hot hand around my shaft.

I groaned and tipped my forehead against hers. "How are we going to get it on? I don't want to let you go." There was no thinking straight while she fisted me.

Snatching the packet from me with her free hand, she ripped it open with her teeth. I eased back enough for her to work between us and roll it on.

Now. Her leggings. Together, we maneuvered her enough to free a leg without me letting her go.

I wanted to impale her, but as ready as I was, I had to make sure it wouldn't be painful for her. Stroking her center, I didn't have to worry. Her slickness coated my fingers. We both needed this.

I dragged myself through her delicious heat and thrust inside.

Her arms came back around me and without missing a beat, she rocked herself on me. The hold of her legs was so tight, I could barely thrust, which was for the best. A few full strokes and I'd be done. This moment reinforced how truly good it'd been the last time. It wasn't because of my hiatus from serious dating, or because she was a forbidden woman. It was us. We were good together.

She bounced on me, her breasts rubbing against my chest. "Chris." Her hands twisted in my shirt and she bucked, and I claimed her mouth as I pumped into her. She went liquid, giving over control to me. Her sex tightened and released. She was close.

I clamped my hands on her hips and took over, thrusting so hard she moved up the wall a few inches. I retreated and thrust again. She stiffened and cried out, but I didn't stop. I stroked her core as she shook through her orgasm. Her sexy moans prompted my own climax. I would've yelled loud enough to draw the neighbors' attention, but she swallowed the sound.

We both tumbled down from our peak. My legs were braced and that was the only reason I didn't collapse. I gave her one last lingering kiss before pulling away.

Doubts about what we'd done a minute after I'd arrived assailed me. "I didn't mean to attack you."

Her sultry tone eased my fear. "I'm glad you did. Hungry?"

"Oh, I'm still starving." I helped her regain her feet and I tucked myself back in until I could take care of the condom.

She pointed me to a small bathroom that was the size of the largest one in my place. I dropped my duffel outside the door and ducked in to clean up. The house was nicely decorated but lacked personality. Perhaps I was used to Jaycee's touch all over my home, but Natalia's landscapes and abstract art weren't what I'd pictured in her home.

With her love of sci-fi assassins, I'd expected framed Starfleet ships done in silvers and black. Instead of a dorm-room-geek feel, they would've been in keeping with her sophisticated, contemporary loft aesthetic. We'd gotten a set into the store last year and they'd been purchased within a week. Mara hadn't wanted to restock with identical artwork, preferring to give the customers a unique experience so they felt like they were buying exclusive pieces. So, she and I had searched for similar art. It was out there, and it was quality, and it was definitely not on Natalia's walls.

I stepped out and followed the scent of seasoning and grilled meat. My stomach rumbled. The weekends by myself were usually the time to make what Jaycee didn't like, but when just cooking for one, it often seemed like too much trouble.

"Smells delicious," I called as I looked around.

Tall ceilings, earth-tone walls, and subdued material on the chairs and sofa. The decor came together for a relaxing feel—for a shrink's office. Candles of various heights dotted the shelves with seashells and a dome filled with succulents.

"Thanks." She puttered around a dining room table larger than my entire dining room. "I went for the lemon pepper chicken and orzo. Then I wasn't sure if you were a chicken guy, so I got the sirloin tenderloins and sweet potato. Whatever we don't eat, I can save for leftovers." Standing back, she eyed her work. "I don't cook."

"You mentioned that." I scanned the table. A vase of real orchids was perched in the middle and a table runner done in sunset colors that accented the flowers ran down the length. Natalia had dished the food into real serving bowls and arranged them on one end of the table. Plates—not paper ones, and not chipped—rested in the two spots at the corner so at least I wouldn't have to holler across the table at her like in Michael Keaton's *Batman*. Gleaming silverware and wineglasses topped off the look.

Were those… Yep, cloth napkins.

"Is it over the top?" She worried her pouty lower lip between her teeth.

I shook my head. To go through all that work, even after ordering in, and still worry about what I thought? "I'm thinking that maybe I've been a little *under* the top."

Her hands flared out like she wanted me to stop that train of thought. "No. No, not at all. I... This is my norm. But nothing's wrong with your norm."

"You don't have to go through this effort for me. What do you do when you order in on your own?"

The excitement in her eyes dimmed and her flush from their tryst was all but gone. "I put it on a plate and sit here." She waved to one of the settings.

All by herself and she still sat at the table? But I was making her nervous and didn't know why. I also didn't know why she didn't just eat from the to-go container while watching Netflix, but that was supposedly a bad habit, albeit what I did when Jaycee was gone. "This one's my spot then?"

Crossing to the chair she usually sat in, I pulled it out for her.

She shot me a quick smile and let me seat her.

We each picked a little of everything. She asked about my work. I asked about her work. It was...awkward.

"This place came furnished," she blurted, then tucked her head down and stabbed a piece of chicken with her fork.

"That makes sense. This didn't seem to be your style."

She cocked her head, her fork poised in midair. "What's my style?"

I waved my arm around. "This is Ms. Shaw's style. I expected your home to have more color. Like maroon."

A blush tinted her cheeks. "It's one of my favorites, obviously."

"Or even a flag from your derby team."

She didn't look at me. "Maybe after I play a full season."

Meekness was a side of Natalia I hadn't anticipated. Certainly not in her own home. At the con, she'd dished out parenting advice. In her office, she'd punished my daughter with professional disregard of who I was to her and what we'd done together. And on the rink, she'd been unstoppable even after she'd crashed.

"Is this a temporary situation?" My heart constricted when I recalled her mentioning that she was a fixer of sorts for Preston Academies.

She sighed and pushed her plate away, the last piece of chicken still impaled on the fork that rested on her plate. "Yes and no. I have an image to maintain."

"But it's your home."

She smiled sadly. "And if my parents ever visit, I don't care to explain all my hobbies. They wouldn't understand. Renting a townhouse gets enough inquiries."

"What the hell are you supposed to live in?"

She hadn't mentioned her parents often, and I was getting a sense why. They were loaded, with the attitude of old money. Minneapolis wasn't an area afflicted with affluent social circles adhering to strict Old-World mores. Rich people yes, but of the modern variety. But having attended Preston myself, I knew they were there. Lower in numbers but represented with all their snooty comments and judgment-filled looks.

"Why rent when you can buy?" Natalia said. She stood, but I leaned over and put a hand on her arm.

"I just hate to see you not be yourself in your own home."

Her expression grew serious. "This is myself, don't doubt that. I had nannies and drivers, and my parents' role was to mentor in the ways of our status. My destiny has always been the academy. It's my family's responsibility, and I'm an only child like my father was."

Her words sunk in. "A teacher and principal were never what you wanted to be."

"I've never…" She licked her lips, and it should've been a distractingly sexy move, but this conversation was too heavy. I thought I knew her, but she had an identity for every facet of her life. "I've never taught."

"Then how—"

"How'd I become a principal, right?" She heaved out a breath. "Yes, we try to keep that part under wraps. I have the necessary education; the rest is at the mercy of the private school. I couldn't waste time teaching when there were schools in need of a leader."

"So, you wanted to teach?"

She lifted a shoulder. "I think it would've been fun, but it was never in my career plan."

One, her grand plan wasn't hers. Two, she probably didn't let herself think of it much because she couldn't teach. She had a destiny.

And I was sending my daughter to this oppressive environment?

Right. I didn't have the money to fight Nana and Papa.

I thought about the career I'd left behind, one I'd worked my ass off for and now barely thought about. "I guess sometimes we have to move with the needs of our family." I almost said, *maybe it works out for the better,* but that didn't seem comparable in her case.

"Yes. And my parents weren't tolerant of outside pursuits based on fictional worlds and characters. But acceptance into extracurricular activities wasn't easy when I was the granddaughter of the founder and the daughter of the owner. I didn't have the skill or the charisma to win over the other kids."

Thus, the mask she put on for everyone else, including Valaria and Shaw Shank.

I stacked my plate on hers. We'd hardly dented the food, but I wasn't ready to ditch our talk to clean up. "When I transferred to the school, I had the people skills and it didn't matter. I hated leaving my friends, but it was nice to just play and have a little more one-on-one attention in the classroom."

She stared at me, her mind whirring in those solid brown eyes. "Do you think your scholarship was necessary?"

"I was a better player than the rest of the team, so yeah, since they wanted to improve, they needed me. But my parents couldn't have afforded a private school, so the scholarship was necessary. Did it help prep me for college? I have no doubt. But that didn't mean I could afford the Ivy League education my classmates got. And I might've been good at high school ball, but I wasn't good enough to score a full ride to one of those schools." I waved it off. "I was a proud Gopher, but I was relegated to rec ball if I wanted to play. I got a good education, so it all worked out."

Her lips pursed. "That's the thing. Preston Academy's traditional attitude equates sports skill with professional success, and they've poured so much money into their football, basketball, lacrosse, and rowing programs—and except for the girls basketball team they only started ten years ago, they're all male dominated."

Ah yes. Jaycee mentioned the same observations. She'd played volleyball in middle school, but Preston didn't have a team. Then there was the lack of fine arts options at the school.

"It's going to be a hard attitude to change," I said.

Natalia snorted. "You're telling me. I dropped the idea of incorporating a general art track, starting with a basic visual arts class next fall and…" She rolled her eyes. "But to do that, we'd need to reallocate money and the football coach is out trying to recruit two players for full rides. Four years of tuition times two and we could have started two classes and sent the teachers to additional training. Not to mention that after the last principal's embezzling, I think we should suspend all attempts at recruitment until we get through the full fallout."

"I thought the board hired you to make those changes."

She reached for her water and took a sip, then washed down a larger mouthful like she found the whole discussion sour tasting. "Oh yes. But once the parents catch wind, they attack the school board. Some of them are friends or run in the same social circles. The last school I was at, they held strong, but my suggestions weren't quite as radical. This time, the guy I just replaced did a number on the school. It's ugly."

"I'm sorry" was all I could say. I didn't envy her job.

"How about we don't talk about work or my parents anymore?"

"Deal. I have something I want to ask you." Her answering grin was cautious, and it should be. I wasn't sure how she'd take what I asked. "Arcadia is having their Christmas party the weekend before New Year's. Care to join me? Jaycee will be going as well."

Natalia didn't respond right away. My heart sank at her lack of enthusiasm. We were dating. Sort of officially. I wanted to do more than sit on the couch and watch movies, or take turns fucking at each other's place once a month.

"We have it after-hours on a Saturday," I explained. "Close the store, have the food catered, and just talk and play games without having to stop to help customers."

She nodded slowly. Was she coming around to the idea? "That's a few weeks away. Who all is going to be there?"

"All of us employees and our families, some close customers who've helped with the business, and the guy that built the place will bring his family. I dunno, maybe twenty people. It's pretty informal. Fun, but informal."

"Can I let you know closer to the day?"

It was three weeks away. "I might have to ask the other deadly derby assassin I'm dating."

Her chuckle was the most genuine response I'd had from her since her orgasm. "My parents haven't informed me of their plans for Christmas. They might be coming here, or I might fly to Seattle. If I'm around, I'd love to go."

I read between the lines. If she was around, and they weren't, then she'd go. It wasn't the answer I'd hoped for, but I'd take it. Extending the invite to my parents was on my lips, but my intuition suggested I wasn't ready for her reaction. I should be used to not being good enough for the families of Preston Academy.

atalia

I STARED at the message on my phone. *Can you make it?*

Arcadia's Christmas party. And my parents were in town. They didn't plan to fly out until after the new year. They were the reason I'd spent the last week of holiday break at work. Thankfully, they'd stayed at a hotel—room service and housekeeping. But I couldn't escape my dad at work, either.

He was wandering the empty halls of Preston while I ran numbers for a fine-arts track versus the number of full-ride scholarships we had to satisfy. Father was probably gloating over the trophies proudly displayed across from the main entrance. He'd no doubt comment on how they'd gone down over the last few years.

I would point him to the former principal, but I had no plans to pursue any regional, district, or state trophies— participation ribbons weren't even on my agenda. My main concern was getting the school to be less reliant on the donations and the insinuations that came with them, and that meant cutting down on the sports scholarships and working with the talent of current and prospective students. Not recruited students.

When I'd approached the board before Christmas break with the outline of my plan, they'd stared at me like I was proposing to recruit super villains to fight crime—until I'd whipped out the figures the new accountant had come up with for me.

Next month, I planned to offer up a list of opportunities we could provide to the students with the funds we did receive from the families and estates of former alums. Fine-arts courses. Study abroad. Exchange programs. I knew which ones I preferred and which ones would appeal to the school board, and unfortunately, they weren't the same.

My office door opened, and my dad strolled in. One hand was stuffed in his charcoal slacks. He was dressed casually today with a cream, cowl-neck, cashmere sweater and a maroon undershirt for a pop of subdued and acceptable color. His trimmed salt-and-pepper hair was cropped short and his stern expression was relaxed for once. He'd gotten the same educational background as me but had never taught a day in his life—like me. He'd spent most of his time traveling from school to school to wine and dine those with deep pockets and make sure their bottom line was satisfied. My mother's schooling had been forgotten, her role relegated to charming hostess with a well of intelligence. Mom was the epitome of the refined and well-bred woman donors wanted their daughters to become or wanted their sons to marry.

Meanwhile, I had been relegated to our home in Seattle, being raised by hired employees. What a goal.

"It's a fine establishment." Father's voice had dropped low, and sometimes I wondered if it was an affectation. When he conversed with Mother, he didn't have a deep voice. Within the school walls—baritone.

"Yes. It has good bones."

His small frown made me regret not enthusiastically agreeing. "Did you know a graduate from a decade ago is in the senate?"

My heart seized. Was he talking about Chris? No. Chris's time was more than a decade in the past, and his election as a state senator wouldn't impress my father enough.

"I'm not surprised." I snagged my glasses off the desk and dropped them in a drawer before Father asked when I'd started wearing them. If he noticed. He wouldn't approve of me needing something other than my last name and good breeding to be taken seriously and changing my last name had been the battle of a lifetime.

"His picture is in the trophy case. He was quarterback, went on to play at West Point, and is now a senator." Pride rang in Father's voice, like he was taking credit for the kid's experience at the academy. What did he tell people about me?

I had never played sports, but I'd sewn my own costume for Halloween once, closed up in my closet while my parents slept—if they were home. Too bad I hadn't gotten to wear it. My mother had asked *Wonder Who?* and made me change before the black-tie Halloween party. Would he say, *she went to college in Washington and is a principal now. She has to wear glasses when she talks to men or they take a few points off her IQ and think she's too young to take seriously. The dimple—it throws them off.*

I needed to go to bed early tonight. I'd been defaulting to my alter ego less and it showed in my bitchy internal monologue. Father was proud of me. I was the fixer, after all—not that he admitted any of the schools had faults, only that I improved on perfection.

Chris was waiting for my answer. Looking at the time, I still had a nice window to get home, change, and meet him at Arcadia. It all depended on what Father and Mother were going to do.

Thankfully, Father didn't make me wait long. "An old classmate's in town. He and his wife invited us to their place tonight. I'm sure you're fine with what you're wearing, but we could head to the hotel to pick your mother up."

Tan slacks, red pumps, and a red sweater that shouldn't itch so much for what it cost? Yeah, I'd loved to socialize in this outfit.

I really wanted to see Chris. Hell with it. "I have plans tonight." Father raised his neatly trimmed brows. Was he surprised? "Are you and Mother okay without me?"

The familiar disapproving frown pulled at Father's mouth. "I think William would love to hear what's going on with the academy. His sons are your age, and he's anxiously waiting for his grandchildren to attend."

"You can fill him in." Surprise flickered across Father's face. It wasn't usual that I breezed past his wishes. "But I committed to a holiday party with a friend before you and Mother called. I'd hate to go back on my word."

Father used to love saying *A man's word is all he has.* I used to mentally fill in *unless he has money,* but I never dared say it out loud. My parents thought of bank accounts as a measure of prestige.

"Very well. We will grab you for brunch tomorrow and I'll pass on any ideas William has for the school."

Yes, because who else would know better what the academy needed than someone who hadn't done more than write annual checks and have drinks with the owner?

Please. But I was off the hook for tonight. As I gathered my purse and phone, I shot back a confirmation to Chris.

My phone pinged when I was locking up the office.

Father was well on his way down the wide corridors to the staff entrance. I peeked at the message, not bothering to hide the smile I got when hearing from Chris in any form. Even better, I'd spend the evening with him and his friends. I hadn't officially met any of them, but from his stories I could probably identify each one. Even better, they didn't care what my profession was or how frivolous my interests were. I didn't have enough people like that in my life.

Great. Pick you up at seven?

I paused. He wanted to pick me up. Then he'd drop me off and probably come inside because maybe he was just as desperate for my touch as I was for his. It'd been three weeks since we'd last had sex and while just seeing him was nice enough, the thought of spending time in his arms catapulted this school break to the best one ever.

I punched in a reply, *Seven it is*, and rushed to catch up with Father.

We parted ways at the parking lot. Father needed to change, and Mother was probably in her Louboutins and pearls, with a pencil skirt two inches past her knees, and her outfit accented in red or green to be properly festive.

I rushed home and sprinted through the shower. I toweled off and dried my hair into a sleek, straight do, then went to stand at my closet, frowning. What should I wear? Since when had I worried about my attire? Sweats to derby practice. Valaria to cons. The same clothes I wore to work also served for meetings, and I dressed like Mother if I had to suffer through any stuffy social function. My current what-to-wear conundrum was whether or not to upgrade Valaria or come up with a new character altogether because it gave me an excuse to bust out my sewing machine.

Leggings, leggings, or jeans? What if I should wear slacks? No, I'd never seen Chris in anything but jeans. My heart pattered when I pictured him in a snug suit, tailored to his tall, lanky, but muscular frame. No wonder he'd gotten elected to office. Dressed up, he would've appealed to the politically driven crowd and the folks who were invested in politics but too busy to deal with the bullshit.

And none of that gave me ideas. The party was at Arcadia. Racks of pop culture clothing ran through my mind. They couldn't be too formal.

Butterflies flitted through my stomach as I stepped into black leggings. Next, I selected a long, cream-colored sweater. Holding it up, I lifted a brow. Was I channeling my father in this outfit? I couldn't deny his confidence in any setting.

The doorbell rang. Damn, he was early. I tossed on the sweater and stuffed my feet into supple knee-high brown boots.

Scurrying down the stairs, I swore as I passed the clock. Had I wasted that much time worrying about what to wear?

I could call Valaria my alter ego, but she was a made-up character with one outfit.

Whipping the door open, I grinned and froze. Out of the corner of my eye, Chris's car was visible in my driveway. Jaycee was climbing into the back seat. So, no sex tonight. I'd forgotten it wasn't the grandparents' weekend.

But a night with Chris and Jaycee was better than any other I'd normally have.

My gaze landed back on him. His winter coat was zipped, but he wore his usual jeans. Only instead of athletic shoes, loafers were on his feet. Quality footwear, probably a throwback to his young, single, professional days.

"You look good," he said, the gleam in his eyes clear. If we didn't have an underage chaperone, he would've slept over tonight.

"Thanks. Let me grab my coat." I darted around the door

to the closet. My hand paused over a dressy, long, black coat. Too much?

Why did standing out in Chris's crowd bother me?

I selected a North Face winter coat instead. Its powder-blue shell with white insert and accents didn't go with my attire, but I had warm mittens in the pockets. Practical. Just like Valaria—with three extra layers.

I hopped into Chris's toasty vehicle.

On the way to the store, Jaycee leaned into the gap between the front seats. "What'd the board say?"

I caught myself before I went *Um...* Putting on my principal persona, albeit slightly softened, I answered, "I'm approaching them next month. I don't know that their priorities align with what we have outlined, but perhaps we can find middle ground."

Chris glanced toward me. His jaw was tight and his eyes dark. He read between the lines.

Jaycee sat back. "Awesome. It'd be such a cool course track. And wouldn't a graphic-art class be a welcome break between AP English and International Business Concepts?"

Jaycee was in neither class, but hypothetically, yes, it'd be a nice break. In the girl's mind, she equated art with easy. It came to her naturally. I would've relished an art or literature class, but my mind was naturally geared toward international marketing techniques and political science.

Who'd Jaycee get her talent from?

To change the subject before Jaycee's hopes rose as high as Tony Stark's tower, I asked what they'd been doing for vacation. We chatted until the beacon that was Arcadia lit up the night.

Green lights lined the front windows of the store and a massive evergreen tree took center stage, lit in red. I had been in last week to update the roller derby flyer and grab more face paint—and get costume ideas for my next cosplay creation. The tree had the best ornaments. Mara and Chris had to have bought out the state in superhero-themed ornaments.

After we parked and rushed in from the cold, another tree graced the entrance. It had been loaded with ornaments that listed a charity and a dollar amount. The tree was bare, except for red-and-blue garland. Justice League or Captain America colors?

"Ooh, all the donations were taken?" I unzipped my coat as warmth surrounded me in spicy fragrant air. The catering had arrived, and my stomach rumbled in response to the savory smells.

"A lot." Chris held his hand out for my coat. I shrugged out of it. "Wes took the rest."

"Wow. That was nice." And I'd only taken one. I could've filled the requests of the whole tree, too. Why hadn't I thought to offer?

Jaycee raced by us, a sketch pad clutched in her hand, and disappeared around the corner. A chorus of voices greeted her. How many people were here?

Chris chuckled. "Flynn's sister Lynne enjoys Jaycee's work. And Jaycee enjoys showing it off."

"It'd be a shame to keep it private." I squared my shoulders. Chris wound his arm around my waist and steered me toward the party.

I was going to tremble out of my boots. Where were my unshakeable nerves? I wore skintight costumes in public. With a mask, but still. I careened around a track and elbowed other women out of my way. I stared down mutinous kids and their imposing parents.

This was so much harder. These people cared about Chris. They were invested in who he dated. This was new territory. I hadn't been groomed for personal relationships. My former last name was usually enough to win over my date's parents.

A small sea of faces greeted me. I recognized Mara and Wes. Wes could make ovaries melt the way he hovered close to his wife and propped his little boy on his shoulder. Mara's dark hair was streaked with green, her little black dress adorned with a bold yellow bat on the front.

I wanted one of my own.

"Hey!" Mara's wide smile instantly relaxed me, but I stayed hugged into Chris's side as he made introductions.

"Over there by the lasagna is Flynn. He built Arcadia, and his wife Tilly bought and paid for him fair and square."

Flynn nodded at us, his hands full of plates and utensils. The woman next to Flynn turned. She was wearing a tight shirt over a round baby belly. In pink letters on her shirt was *We're hoping for a Warrior Princess*. Her grin could power Arcadia's lights. "He was worth every penny."

I chuckled. "I've heard the story." Chris had said he'd narrowly missed the bachelor auction, He had shamelessly used Jaycee as his excuse.

Mara sat next to an older woman in a motorized wheelchair who was laughing. The gentleman beside her had the stiff posture that came with wearing a suit all day. No slouching allowed.

"It's almost more salacious than our story," Mara said. "This is my mom, Wendy, and one of our most faithful customers, Ephraim. He sued my husband for me."

"I tried," the man said in a deep timbre. Wendy lifted her hand in greeting.

Jaycee was parked next to another woman in a standard, unmotorized wheelchair.

Chris steered me next to Jaycee. "Lynne, this is Natalia, the woman I told you about." He leaned down and said in a conspiratorial whisper, "The assassin."

Chris had said Lynne was nonverbal, but since Flynn had

been back in her life and in charge of her care, they'd all been learning some basic signs Lynne could do with her functional arm. I got a thumbs-up.

"Nice to meet you." I peeked over Jaycee's shoulder at the pad in front of Lynne on the table. My eyes widened at the page the sketchbook was open to. The pencil drawing of Lynne was in black and white, but the detail put into the woman's hair, clothing, and even her wheelchair was at a level that not many fourteen-year-olds possessed. "That's stunning."

Lynne ducked her head.

Jaycee shrugged. "The others seem embarrassed when I sketch them. Not Lynne. We're planning a canvas for her room, but I need to practice on a smaller scale first."

If Chris's heart wasn't going to burst with pride, mine would. This was the rebellious, obnoxious girl in my office at the beginning of the year? And she didn't suddenly turn this corner. Jaycee might spend one weekend a month with her grandparents, and have a meal or two with her mother, but these people at Arcadia were her family.

I swallowed and glanced around. Flynn carried two plates loaded with food to a spot across from Lynne and Jaycee. His wife was articulating with her hands and laughing over the story she told. At the neighboring table, Mara had just taken her son to the restroom with a giant maroon-and-black tote thrown over her shoulder. Were those Deadpool eyes stitched into the side?

Wes had joined the conversation with Wendy and Ephraim. Chris led me to the food table. I went through the motions of picking and choosing lasagna, salad, and—was that cheesecake? I carried my plate to a separate table and sat. As Chris took his chair next to me, Ephraim turned. "I found a vintage Axis & Allies on eBay."

The two men delved into a conversation I couldn't follow.

Board games weren't my thing. I picked at my food and looked around. The party was informal, comfortable, a way for everyone to connect without the interruption of daily life. So different than any gathering I had ever experienced.

And I felt horribly out of place.

Chris

I POKED around in a cupboard at Natalia's place. I'd thought I was going to have to wait another week before I could spend a night with her, but Mara and Wes hadn't seen the newest *Star Wars* movie and Jaycee had offered to babysit and she'd just spend the night at their place. I hoped it'd give me a chance to ask Natalia if anything was wrong, and I had, but she'd brushed me off. And once we were here and naked, well, talking wasn't what either of us were interested in.

I focused on the sad contents of the shelves. Rye toast, tins of tuna, and packets of shredded chicken with their own crackers that had actual flax seeds on the surface. I must be out of touch with the cracker world.

Switching to the fridge, I searched for something I could make us for breakfast. Who didn't even have eggs?

Greek yogurt, something called kefir, and an assortment of already-sliced fruits and vegetables stocked the fridge.

Froufrou crackers and fruit then. I couldn't stomach yogurt, but I'd grab her a container.

The doorbell rang and I jumped, letting the appliance door swing shut.

I rounded the corner of the kitchen. Natalia had sprinted to the top of the landing, a sheet wrapped around her, ready to trip her if she attempted the stairs. Her hair was as wild as her expression.

"Oh my god. I forgot about brunch. My parents!"

The panic in her face didn't make sense, but maybe getting caught with a guy at any age wasn't something a kid wanted to do. At least they hadn't walked in on me in the kitchen like I was stuck in the Groundhog Day episode of *Supernatural*. Only instead of watching Dean die over and over, I was repeatedly busted half naked with Natalia.

I was about to suggest I let them in, but I was in nothing but boxers.

"Just a minute," Natalia shouted. Her frantic gaze swiveled from the front door to me. "You're naked."

"Nearly. Let me get dressed." I jogged up the stairs. By the time I reached the second floor, Natalia had disappeared into the bedroom. More clothing littered the floor than before. A Preston sweater had already been pulled over her head and she was dancing around on one foot to get into the black leggings I'd peeled off her hours ago.

"Brunch. Dammit." She tore out of the room.

My gaze lingered on the doorway for a moment before I picked through the items on the floor to find my clothing. I was in my thirties, but flashbacks of my time with Cierra ran through my mind, her terror that her parents would find out we were dating. It was like she'd thought she'd be disowned if her parents discovered we were sleeping together. It turned out that hadn't been far off the mark.

But Natalia wasn't a scared seventeen-year-old girl. She was independent and had an enviable career. I refused to be ashamed of where I was in my life; I was exactly where I wanted to be. And that included spending the night with her.

Voices drifted upstairs.

"I, um, had a friend over last night." Natalia never lacked

conviction, but she could pass for Jaycee the way she talked to her parents.

"Oh?" That must be her mother. And she didn't sound thrilled. "I was concerned you were going to wear that outfit to the restaurant."

Harsh.

"Well, invite him along." Natalia's dad. "I have a reservation at Nicolette Island Inn. It should be no problem to accommodate another."

"Uh…"

I paused at the top of the stairs and waited for the rest of her response.

"I'm not sure he can make it." Natalia's back came into view. She had herded her parents away from the entry to where they couldn't see the stairs.

I descended, my stocking feet not making a sound. My back straight, proud, I turned the corner. Natalia wasn't facing me. Her parents noticed me first. Had they ever worn a stitch of denim in their life? The way her mother's manicured eyebrows rose and her gaze drifted down me, growing more dismayed as it went, probably not.

Natalia's father was dressed in slacks and shoes that cost more than any pair in my closet, and I still had every pair I'd ever bought that weren't athletic shoes. The black peacoat the man wore was trendy and kept him from looking older than his sixty-ish years. Given the more traditional threads Natalia's mom was sporting, his choice was probably a style risk in their world.

Natalia spun around. "Chris. Mother, Father, this is Chris Halliwell."

Her father stepped around her and extended his hand. "Bertram Preston." My heart stammered at the last name. Natalia's family really were the owners and founders of that damn school. "This is my wife, Carina. Halliwell, you said?"

Carina politely inclined her head, but she kept her hands tucked into her front pockets as she assessed him. A flash of understanding hit me—this was why Natalia acted the way she did in various situations. She and her mother were nothing alike. Or were they more alike than either imagined?

Natalia put her hand on my shoulder. "Chris is an alum of Preston, actually."

Approval lit Bertram's eyes and Carina's body language softened, if only going from as rigid as lead to as hard as steel.

I smiled, summoning the charm I reserved for winning customers and suppliers over. "Yes. I was awarded a basketball scholarship."

Bertram's eyes crinkled at the corners. "And I'm sure the trophies are proudly displayed. What do you do now?"

Natalia jumped at the answer before I could. "He's a business owner."

I leveled my gaze on her. Guilt flashed in her eyes, but at least she had enough conscience not to hide it.

I was good enough in bed, but not good enough for her family.

No. I wasn't playing this game. Not again.

I met Bertram's gaze. "I co-own a comic book and gaming shop." I could mention that their daughter was a customer, but that wasn't my fight. If she wanted to hide parts of herself from the various worlds she lived in, that was her issue.

Carina cocked her head like she wasn't sure she'd heard correctly. "A what?"

"The Arcadia. It's a comic book and gaming shop. We also host related events."

"Chris used to be on the—"

I cut Natalia off without looking at her. "It doesn't matter what I used to be. I'm a dad now, and I enjoy my work. Speaking of which, I should go pick up my daughter."

Bertram's brows lifted. "Daughter?"

Why the surprise? Many men my age had children. Or were the Prestons used to having "people" for their children?

"She's a student," Natalia said, her voice soft. "Third generation."

I had to give it to her. She hadn't given up on what was the good fight in her eyes.

"It was nice meeting you both." What a lie.

I stepped away and went in search of my shoes and coat. Thankfully, they were by the garage entrance and out of view of her parents. I sensed Natalia behind me but ignored her as I stepped into my loafers.

"I'm sorry," she whispered.

"Yeah" was all I could say.

I grabbed my coat off the hook and didn't bother throwing it on. She trailed me into the garage but waited until the door shut behind her, blocking us from the couple inside, before she spoke.

"Chris."

I was halfway to the side door. Stopping, I dug my keys out and hit the autostart. I was miserable, but I didn't have to freeze. Facing her, I was staggered by the regret in her eyes. Her parents' judgment was that important to her? So be it.

"Natalia. I've been through this before." I gestured toward the main house. "It doesn't end well for me, and I'm not going to live as your dirty little plebeian secret."

She sighed and pushed her messy hair off her face. It must've killed her to let her mother see her like that. It would've destroyed Cierra. "It's not like that."

I drifted toward her. "Really? So, what—we go back in. I can tell them all about Arcadia and the daughter I had out of wedlock that was so scandalous I thought I'd been teleported to the 1950s. I can give them Nana and Papa's last name and see if it gets me any street cred, though we'll skip the part where I wasn't good enough to become their son-in-law. Then we can go to brunch, where you'll be as mortified as your mother that I'm wearing jeans and a shirt that cost less than fifty dollars. What if the other patrons mistake me for the kitchen staff?" Who would probably be dressed fancier than I was anyway.

"Chris."

I cut my head to the side and held a hand up. "No. I'm not being limited to only one of the dimensions you live in. Goodbye, Ms. Shaw."

atalia

I SLUMPED IN MY CHAIR. Another month, another board meeting. Only this was the meeting I was supposed to bring up the proposal for the fine-arts track. Acid churned in my stomach. The new semester had been going for two weeks and I'd worked twelve-hour days. Mostly to avoid going home.

My phone remained silent. Chris's goodbye had been final. My parents had flown back to Seattle, and my mother had been relieved that the "Chris phase" was over.

He's not son-in-law material. You need a man who can keep up with you.

So ironic. As if Mother hadn't been following Father's coattails all over the country. I had heard my mother admit to barely graduating college because of the travel demands of Father's job. But for status reasons, Mother had needed the Princeton credentials.

My gaze landed on the same diploma hanging on my wall. My mind drifted back to that devastating morning Chris had walked out on me. Could I blame him? I'd tried talking him up to Father, but the attempt had only been an insult. Two different decades, yet Chris had gotten the same treatment. Both of those times in the twenty-first century.

No wonder Valaria was from the future.

A knock at the door saved me from the instant replay that haunted me hourly. Ms. Branson poked her head in. I straightened and wiped the dejected expression from my face. "Come in."

"Douglas Johnson just arrived. All the board members are here."

"Thanks." I grabbed my portfolio. It included stacks of handouts that I'd later email. Not for the first time I wished we had upgraded with the times and had projectors that weren't from my parents' days in school.

I took a moment to check my appearance in the mirror, wishing I were into makeup for more reasons than just cosplay. Dark circles rimmed my eyes, and my pallid skin could use some foundation. My customary bun was fraying after a long day and a billion attempts to run my hands through my hair before remembering how tightly bound I kept it all day.

At least I had my dark-rimmed glasses. The contrast of the frames against my face was enough to prevent me from looking sickly.

"Let's do this," I muttered.

My heels clicked on the polished hardwood all the way to the conference room. The halls were empty, and when I passed the trophy case I slowed. Were one of these from Chris? Most likely. How had I never stopped to find him in the team photos?

Because what if someone asked why I was perusing the sports display? It wasn't like I ever lingered here.

Or was it because I'd realized that scholarships ultimately helped the kids? Physical activities helped students, and I'd been remiss in equalizing the opportunities available to each gender in the school. Or had I been trying to create a divide in my own mind?

Shaking my head, I continued to the room.

Entering the meeting, I kept my chin high, my shoulders back, and my expression cool. Adopting a pleasant smile, I met each board member's eye. They were in charge. The occupants of the room as an entity were my bosses. They supposedly had my back. But with each meeting since I'd started, it became clearer that I didn't have their listening ears, almost like someone else had whispered in them first.

"Ms. Shaw," greeted Henry Tanaka, the president. "How was your holiday?"

Long, boring, ending in heartbreak. "It was well. The same for all of you, I hope."

Murmurs of agreement rippled through the room as I sat at the opposite end of the long mahogany table from Henry. The meeting ran smoothly. I'd been in sessions that had grown passionate and heated. Emotions could run high in the business of education. We weren't acquiring artifacts or shuffling money in accounts; we were educating our future.

Finally, we reached my agenda items.

I passed the worksheets down and refrained from pushing up my glasses. Nerves of steel. "I've noted that previous Preston Academies, and this one in particular, lack a basic fine-art track in the curriculum. A student who's interested in seeing Preston offer more in that area offered to gather data, and I ran the numbers."

"Art?" Claudia Ortega and derision were never far apart. I never knew if the woman was friend or foe. Claudia probably said the same thing about me. Of the board of five, Claudia was the only female. I had initially suspected she'd been a huge proponent of my hiring. But now I doubted it. I'd read the notes, and Henry had been the swing vote for the divided board.

"Yes." I could quote the benefits of an art program, but the notes were attached to the spreadsheet. I'd send an email afterward. Hammering the point home any more would reek of desperation and this was a group that'd feed off of it.

"How does this fit into our mission?" Claudia asked, her dark head tipped as she paged through the document.

Murdock, a burly man who towered over all of them even seated, spoke. "We don't want to graduate students who are fleeing to Hollywood to hit it big, or gallivanting through New York art galleries. We're educating leaders of the world, not the next big thing." He said the last word like that would be the most horrible outcome for any student. Murdock had been a star fullback, running back, something-back in his day.

But are we educating leaders of the world? My notes also compared the expense of all the sports programs combined, and it far exceeded all other program tracks.

I gave in to the urge to adjust my glasses. "A well-rounded student can make a great leader." Lately, I had been thinking we should adjust our mission statement to *paving the way for parents to live vicariously through their children.*

"A focused student can do greater things." This was from Charles, the oldest of the team, and the most steadfastly adherent to old ideals and traditions. He'd been the other "no" vote for hiring me.

"Whose focus? The kids or their parents?" I managed to keep my voice calm and not snap at Charles.

Claudia's head tilted, her gaze assessing.

Charles harrumphed. "If kids could focus themselves,

they wouldn't be kids. They wouldn't be raised by their parents for the first eighteen years of their life and dependent on them for the next four. Preston Academy is here for the families. If we start giving in to children's wants and desires, then we might as well close our doors and shuffle them to public schools."

Murdock shook his head. Henry had stayed quiet, along with the fifth member, Guy.

This wasn't an argument I was going to make any progress in. That was two members of the board who were immediately against my proposal. Guy, Claudia, and Henry weren't likely to agree to big curriculum changes until Charles and Murdock could stew on the information awhile. Or resign.

Guy said my thoughts out loud, though in a more socially correct way. "I certainly think it's something we can look into at a later time." He flipped to a specific page in the report and I knew exactly which one. It was filled with charts and graphs I'd made sure to color code. "What I think needs to garner our attention is the unbalanced and unchecked spending in the extracurricular activities. Is this correct? Our students don't have access to updated technology in the classroom?"

I let out a slow breath. You win some, you lose some. Unfortunately, while researching the technological needs of a fine-arts program, I had come across schools where every student was issued an iPad for the year. Each classroom had an interactive smart board instead of a chalkboard. Some high schools had even done away with textbooks, and they were larger facilities than Preston.

The meeting dissolved into a discussion about what would be the best fit for the school and most seemed to agree with the technology upgrades. Each time my excitement soared, I remembered that I'd have to break the news to

Jaycee, that while the girl's work wasn't for nothing, a fine-arts program wasn't going to happen in the near future.

It didn't matter what role I filled, I couldn't help but disappoint both the father and daughter.

∾

Chris

IT WAS close to Valentine's Day and since even superheroes and fanboys fell in love, I was surrounded by heart-faced emojis while waiting on customers selecting the perfect gift for the geek in their life.

It sucked. I missed Natalia, but the burn of her unknowing rejection hadn't faded. It didn't help when Jaycee came home in tears. Her hopes had been dashed and she was sentenced to three more years lacking stimulation surrounded by kids who didn't "get" her. Add to that the various fine-arts programs in local high schools she'd found, and Jaycee was moping around the house, miserable, and in full teen mode. I thought I'd gone through the worst during the last two years with her moods, but no.

My cell phone rang but I ignored it. Customers roamed the aisles and if anyone really needed to get ahold of me, they had my work number.

I finished ringing up one of our regular customers and her stack of *Lucifer* pulls. The woman's hair was dyed platinum and the way her pale face glowed under the store's combo of natural and fluorescent lights, I guessed she was trying to pull off her own *iZombie* look.

The store phone rang, and I froze, handing off the bag to the lady. First my personal phone and now the store? Not a coincidence. I plastered a smile on my face. "Enjoy."

Two more rings went by before I grabbed the receiver.

"Arcadia Comics. Can I help you?" My heart pounded. Was Jaycee in trouble again? Would it be her on the other end?

"Hi, Chris." Natalia's words lacked her Ms. Shaw crispness. Instead, her resignation traveled through the line.

"What's wrong." I didn't say it like it was a question. Natalia wouldn't have tried my private phone and then the store if she were calling to beg to see me again, or if Jaycee had nailed student of the year. Not that Preston Academy had a student of the year. They were all supposed to be exceptional, all the time.

"Jaycee skipped her morning classes and has violated the dress code once again. I'm afraid she'll face the next round of disciplinary measures." Natalia sucked in a breath. "Which is expulsion."

"For skipping?" The news hit my gut like a punch from Hellboy. "I get that she's violated the rules a few times, but it was for pretty tame stuff, for normal kid stuff."

"Yes, but Preston Academy holds its students to a higher standard."

"Fuck Preston Academy." Two of the closest customers lifted their heads above the aisle. Dammit. "Sorry," I called, and into the phone, I apologized again. "Sorry, Natalia. She can't get expelled. Her grandparents…"

"I understand, Chris. Can you come into the office so we can outline the consequences and what it'll mean for Jaycee?"

Mara was in the back and she'd cover for me, but it was the third time this school year I'd ditched her. "Yeah, I'll be right there."

I darted down the hall by the register and knocked on Mara's oak-stained office door. "Hey. Jaycee struck again and I have to go to the school. Can you cover?"

"Of course." Mara was out of her seat before I finished. "I hope everything's okay."

My look must've portrayed my frustration with my daughter and my spiking anxiety about whether her grandparents would follow through with their threat to fight me for custody. I'd sent Jaycee to Preston like they wanted. Whether she walked the line to stay there was out of my power. I couldn't sit on her twenty-four hours a day, and no one should expect me to when they took such a small role in her life.

The twenty-five-minute drive to the school felt like an hour. The bitter wind bursting through the trees around the building matched my mood. Striding through the front entrance and straight to the office, I couldn't produce much of a greeting. The administrative staff recognized me by now and waved to the left where Ms. Shaw's corner office was hidden away. Just as the woman inside hid herself from the world.

Jaycee was slumped in a chair across from Ms. Branson's sturdy desk. Her cheeks were red and blotchy, and tears brimmed in her eyes, ready to fall. My gaze dipped to her jeans and Vans. How'd I miss that this morning?

No. She'd been in khaki pants, with the same emerald top, and had remarked on the brutal cold and how grateful she was she didn't have to walk to school or go outside between classes.

I sighed and she looked up. Ms. Branson ducked her blond head to give us a feeling of privacy. I wasn't going to make my drama public any more than it already was. I bypassed Ms. Branson and barged into Natalia's office.

Ms. Branson's chair scraped back, and she squeaked like she was going to say something, but I'd already disappeared inside and closed the door behind me. Natalia jerked her head up. A sheet of paper was in front of her, and her keyboard had been pushed out of the way.

I didn't take my eyes off her as I crossed to the seat. A stronger man could've looked away and she was my weakness. Her hair was bound, and she reached for a black-rimmed pair of glasses, but her hand stalled over them.

My mind flashed back to the first time I'd been in this office. She'd worn those, but I hadn't seen them on her since. And she didn't wear contacts.

Really? Glasses? Was she ever the real Natalia Preston Shaw with anyone?

I plopped into the chair, rested my elbows on the armrests, and clasped my hands in front of my stomach. "Lay it on me."

Pushing her chair away from her desk, she crossed her legs and I wanted to groan. Did she have to pick a skirt to wear today of all days? She hadn't known Jaycee would decide to be a little delinquent today. The skirt was part of her Ms. Shaw identity. Sharp. Professional. But with a kick of femininity the men she worked with couldn't deny, like her own little rebellion. Natalia wasn't a business-skirt woman. She was a sweats-and-leggings woman, but "they" had expectations so she must live up to them.

Natalia tilted her head. Was my resentment streaming through my features? Probably. I had Nana and Papa to deal with. Would they live up to their threats? I'd been in Jaycee's life full-time for four years. Yet, Cierra had all the power. I should've fought for custody when I had the means, but her parents had already been murmuring in her ear, convincing them a nanny would be just as good. An informal deal, an understanding between me and Cierra, had seemed suffi-cient and also wouldn't make Jaycee feel like her mother had totally given up on her. Which was the truth, wasn't it? But at the time, I'd been willing to absorb the hard feelings and stress to buffer my daughter.

"I went through the policy in detail before you got here." Natalia flipped the document in front of her around and pushed it across the desk. I didn't bother reaching for it. "Jaycee will be expelled for the rest of the year. However, upon proof of completion of ninth grade at another school and an essay about what she learned about her time away from Preston, she can petition to return to the school for her sophomore year."

I dropped my gaze from her steady one to glare at the paper. Expelled. My daughter. "Natalia. I'm going to lose her if you do this."

She pressed her lips together. Sympathy simmered in her eyes, but so did determination. "I'm really sorry, Chris. I think Jaycee's going to continue to struggle with the board's decision to table the new course track, and I anticipate that she will continue to act out."

I couldn't look at her. Was I expecting her to bend rules for me just because we slept together?

Yeah, I kinda was. But also because Natalia knew what was riding on this decision and she wasn't allowing one inch of leeway for Jaycee.

Natalia leaned forward. "There's only three months left in this school year. She can use the time away to work through her feelings and finish her freshman requirements. I'm sure she'll get back in next year."

Get back in next year. That sounded awful.

"You know what? I want her nowhere near this place." Now that I'd admitted it, the floodgates opened. "What has Preston ever done for her? As a matter of fact, what has anyone who's had anything to do with Preston ever done for her? Her mother gave her up. Her grandparents force this vile place on her like it's her greatest wish to spend her days with other kids who only care about what she can do for them. Her teachers only pay attention to her when she breaks the goddamn precious rules." *And I didn't swoop in to defend her needs.* The anger roiling in me redirected itself toward Natalia. "And you made her think she could actually make a difference among these people."

Natalia's lips pursed. "The fact is—and this was hard for me to reconcile with, too—this school works for many families. We stick to the mission statement and we graduate kids who are leaders."

"Leaders of what?" I sat forward. "What kind of leaders, Natalia? I'm sorry, we're supposed to pretend we weren't an item, right? *Ms. Shaw.* What leaders? You need to redefine that mission statement because it's deceptively narrow. Jaycee has no inclination to be a bank president or a politician, but that's all Preston cares about." Her expression brimmed with shock, but I wasn't done. "And I don't think this place is where Jaycee will learn to be comfortable with herself, with me, or with the world. I don't want her hiding behind a mask or-or"—my gaze landed on her frames —"glasses."

Natalia flinched like I'd shoved her despite the heavy desk between us. I ground my jaw down before irritation over our breakup spilled into the argument. Like it hadn't already.

"You're right." My gaze lifted to hers. Had she really said that? "Maybe Preston isn't for Jaycee. But insulting those it is for is low. Bringing up my personal history is… Well, your need to please Cierra's parents is not Preston Academy's problem." She flattened her hands on the smooth top of her desk. "Your mistake regarding Jaycee's custody and your terror of its repercussions are understandable. But don't throw how I behave around my family into this, not when you've done nothing but go against your best instincts to make Nana and Papa happy. Don't come to me when your daughter does what she wants, not when you've been letting her do what she wants whenever she's around you."

I... What? Was this her version of *you do you*? Her censorious words from the first day we met coursed through my mind. She was the boss, used to people jumping when she said so. She was educated and entitled. None of that meant she knew it all. "It's easy to be an armchair expert. You've read all the textbooks, taken all the classes. But you haven't taught. You haven't been a parent. Come to me with your opinion when you actually have experience."

I popped up and stormed out. She might've called my name, but blood was pounding between my ears. Was the woman who'd been raised in an ivory tower saying I spoiled my daughter?

"Come on, Jaycee. Let's clean out your locker and get going." I strode out, Jaycee's footsteps rushing behind me.

The halls were empty, thank God. I gestured to Jaycee to lead the way. We cleaned out her locker, leaving all the textbooks behind. Jaycee sniffled and refused to meet my eyes. I shouldered her backpack and marched back to the exit.

After we were loaded and pulling away, I checked the rearview mirror. I wouldn't lie. Seeing the brick monster fade in the distance was satisfying. My time there hadn't been the high point of my life, and that school had made my daughter miserable. And if Natalia ever peeled back that armor she'd constructed around her, she'd see it was doing the same to her.

A serious conversation was required with Jaycee, but I couldn't summon the basic question of "What were you thinking?" We drove in silence for a few minutes.

My phone vibrated. Seriously. What now? "Yeah?"

"Mr. Halliwell, this is Ms. Branson from..."

My joyful afternoon wasn't done yet. "Yep." What now?

"There was a form we needed you to sign to show we've gone over the policy with you."

Natalia's slender fingers pushing the paper across her desk flashed through my mind. Damn. "And verbal's not good enough?"

"Unfortunately not."

"You have my address. Throw it in the mail and I'll get it right back to you."

Her beat of silence was enough warning that I wasn't going to like what she had to say. "Sorry for the inconvenience, Mr. Halliwell, but we haven't had the best of luck with something of this caliber getting returned to us. We really ask that it's signed in person."

And I really ask that I don't have to see Preston again. "Fine. I'll be in tomorrow after five." When I was off work. So Mara wouldn't have to cover for any more of this bullshit. If Nana fought me for custody, I'd be asking all of our employees to cover my ass.

"Thank—"

I hung up and concentrated on driving.

Tomorrow after five meant I had over twenty-four hours to anticipate seeing Natalia again.

But it gave me all of tonight after work to have a comprehensive discussion with Jaycee about what her decisions might cost us.

atalia

THE CLOCK TICKED to 4:50. Butterflies swelled in my stomach until the antipasto turkey sandwich on rye I'd had for lunch threatened to evacuate my body.

Chris was going to be here soon. The rest of the staff had cleared out. Only the janitorial employees were in the building and they started on classrooms first. I often worked late so they saved the offices for last.

I tapped my pen against the desktop. Payroll forms were scattered in front of me, and I'd been staring at them for over an hour. All that was required was my signature and Ms. Branson would forward them to accounting.

But it wasn't just the impending confrontation with Chris that was on my mind. I'd reviewed the footage of Jaycee from the previous day. She'd skipped the morning, and so had Dresden. Jaycee had gotten out of her dad's car, in proper Preston Academy attire, and strode into the school, then backtracked and hopped in with a newly licensed Dresden.

I hadn't called Dresden's parents yet, nor had I approached the teachers who hadn't reported Dresden's absence. Anger burned through me. Jaycee had taken the fall once again, while the reputation of Dresden's parents and his athletic skill protected him.

Fun times to look forward to tomorrow as I called a meeting with the boy, Mr. and Mrs. Wentworth, and the faculty involved, which included Coach Sammie.

I signed off on the payroll and rose. Passing the bookshelf, the prism caught my eye. Days were lengthening this time of year, but a little sun shone into my office. I adjusted the prism so the *S* faced out. It'd catch the light better.

Carrying the forms out of my office to Ms. Branson's desk, I nestled them in the tray by my assistant's desk. This process would get an overhaul if the board approved spending on technology upgrades that'd benefit not only the students, but the staff.

Turning around, I spotted a man. I gasped. "Chris!"

He was in the entry of the main office, his usual easy body language less relaxed and more…worn. Fatigued. Haggard.

But he looked good. His broad shoulders filled the width of the doorway, and his winter coat hung open. His hands were shoved in the pockets of his loose jeans, and his shirt of the day read *My Ring Grants Me Powers. What Does Yours Do?* It would've made me smile if it weren't for how we'd parted yesterday.

He stepped in but didn't cross to me. "Where's this form I need to sign?"

"In my office." I would've brought it out with me if I'd known he was arriving. Walking back into the constraints of my office with him messed with my emotions. There was valid tension between us, and I'd be gutted if he did nothing more than sign and go. But I couldn't let myself be excited about being alone with him.

I could've offered to grab it, but there was something I wanted to mention to him, a detail from the video that bothered me. It could be nothing, but he was Jaycee's father, and the decision about whether it was significant was his.

He hovered between the door and the chair he usually sat in, his brow crinkling when he noticed we were closed in together.

I pointed to my desk where the paper rested with a pen on the side where visitors sat. "Just sign at the bottom, please."

Instead of sitting behind my fortress, I closed the distance between us. He scribbled on the paper and tossed the pen down. His gaze narrowed on me.

"I wanted to talk to you about a concern of mine with Jaycee."

A brow lifted. I took in a shaky breath. Being around him was usually so comfortable. I could argue with him without worrying about what he thought of how I was dressed and whether or not it influenced what he thought of me.

I squeezed my hands together. His gaze dipped down, but his expression didn't fill with gloating. How was he going to react to what I said?

"What has Jaycee told you about yesterday when she skipped?"

We were only a couple of feet apart. He folded his arms and towered over me, but I didn't feel threatened and he didn't have the look of someone using his size for intimidation. The gravity playing through his features spoke of the long talk he must've had with his daughter.

"She said she was upset and couldn't take another day in this place." His voice rumbled over my body. I craved his voice. "According to her, 'it's so basic.'" His statement lacked humor.

"Did she mention who she was with?"

He shook his head. "No. She said she camped out in the bathroom, in clothing that wouldn't repress her free spirit."

"As soon as you drove away, she left with another student."

Chris studied me for a moment. "And I suppose you can't tell me who?"

"No, but I'm going to address his absence tomorrow with his parents." And the staff that didn't report him.

Fire flashed, making the green in Chris's eyes lighten. "A guy? Dresden?"

I pursed my lips to keep from confirming the boy's identity, but Chris didn't push it.

"Are you kidding me? She was alone with him all morning, doing God knows what?" He shoved his hand through his hair. "Shit."

I rested my hand on his chest. He froze under the touch, but I didn't move my hand. He needed to know about Dresden, but my next observation was what bothered me. "You remember when you picked her up, she was wearing jeans?" He nodded. "I... It's just that... Those other times she was tardy, she wore skirts."

A muscle jumped in his jaw. The level of conversations he probably had with his daughter this year weren't for the weak dad.

It wasn't my goal to make him reminisce, so I got to the point. "Jaycee was wearing jeans. It's cold out, and while I'm not around Jaycee a lot, when I was"—when we were together—"she wasn't a jeans girl. She wore leggings. I'm worried that she is getting pressured for more than a few feels in a janitor's closet."

"And jeans were like her armor?"

"It might be stupid." It's not like they would prevent anything sexual from happening, but they'd slow it down more than leggings. "I might be way off the mark. I was her age once. Some guys that age see an insecure girl and think that it's an opening." I shrugged and dropped my hand.

Chris's gaze darkened. "Did you have a Dresden in your life?"

I chuckled, but I couldn't look at him. "I was only fooled once. After that, I made it a policy to not date classmates." I hesitated over the parallel to my adult life. "Anyway, Jaycee and *the boy* had something going on last fall, then there wasn't, and I saw him arm in arm with other infatuated girls. Now, Jaycee's hurting and acting out. Even if he's not fully aware, he senses her weakness and he's probably looking for more than some fondles."

Chris sucked in a breath, his gaze heated. "I'll talk to her. And maybe buy her a few more pairs of jeans."

My lips twitched. The topic was too heavy for laughter, but he was heeding my concerns. Few other parents facing the woman who'd kicked their kid out of school would do the same.

"How's it going with Nana and Papa?" I hadn't meant to broach the sensitive topic that I was the root of, but I couldn't help but worry about him.

His shoulders dropped and he shook his head. "I haven't talked to them yet. I'm going to get Jaycee settled in a new school and then meet with Cierra. She's the one wielding the power whether she wants it or not."

"Do you think she'll talk custody with you without her parents interfering?"

Chris's expression remained somber. "It depends on what they think about her fiancé. If she wants to redirect her focus to make my life miserable while she gets hitched without the drama, then that's what she'll do."

"I'm sorry."

"Yeah," he said quietly.

Without thinking, I stroked his cheek. He looked destroyed. He'd offered everything he could to Cierra, and it hadn't been enough. Then he'd ditched his career for his daughter and it still wasn't enough. I almost said something stupid like, "If there's anything I can do," when clearly, I'd done enough.

Frustration tracked up my spine. The stinking mess of his life had landed at my feet and I'd only been a catalyst, but he blamed me. And I agreed, even if I was just doing my job.

My gaze swept his tired face. His hair was more disheveled than normal, like he'd run his hands through it a few hundred times. But that didn't detract from his attractiveness. A good-looking man who was eaten up with anxiety over his future with his daughter.

"Chris." I couldn't think of more to say. I just wanted to make it better and I didn't know how, and it wasn't my place.

He swayed closer, his head dropping. My breath hitched. Was he going to kiss me? My gaze hooked on his lips. They were parted and a breath away.

I stretched up and met him in the middle. Our mouths crashed together with a stronger force than anticipated. I clutched his shirt to keep my balance. His hands snaked around my waist, turning me until my ass hit the edge of the desk.

Desire roared through me like a lightning bolt, singeing all my good sense with it. I'd missed this man, and he had me in his arms. That was all I cared about.

Clutching him, I pushed closer. Our mouths were open, our tongues tasting, savoring. The ruffling of papers falling to the floor didn't bother me in the slightest.

Oh yes. I'd missed this, how he made me feel, the fire he stoked inside of me.

Prying my hands off him, I slid them under his coat and around his waist, wanting the heat of his skin to seep into me. I curled my fingers around the hem of his shirt and tugged it up.

He mimicked my actions. My shirt was loose in seconds and his fingers skimmed around my waistband like he was searching for the clasp.

Worried he wouldn't find it, I released his top just as he abandoned my waist and bunched up the material of my skirt. Cool air hit my thighs and I widened them to fit around him.

He settled between my legs, the warm denim lighting up my nerve endings as the edges of his coat tickled my shins. More. I needed more. The ache in my center that taunted me each night I fell asleep alone bloomed back to life. For as long as we'd known each other, we hadn't landed in bed as often as other couples with less tangled obligations, but my body was primed for him. I could've stripped down the moment I'd turned and seen his rugged figure in the doorway.

We ground against each other and I let out a whimper. The rigid length behind his fly wasn't enough. Reaching between us, I flipped open the button of his pants.

He groaned when my fingers grazed his shaft. Or was that me? I ripped the two sides apart, not caring if I destroyed the zipper.

He blazed a path across my cheek and down my neck. Separating long enough to give me room to work him free, he released my hips to flick open the top buttons of my shirt. One plastic round loosened and clattered to the floor.

Maybe I should care about being presentable, but my door was shut. I fisted his length. Long and hard, he throbbed in my hand, just as I was doing in his.

He wrestled my shirt open far enough to yank down my

bra. My nipples popped free, like they were reaching for him. I arched back, releasing him to bring my breasts closer to his mouth. He rocked his hips and I strained for him.

Biting my lip, I let my head fall back. His wicked tongue circled my pebbled nipples. Still it wasn't enough. Wiggling, I stroked my sex against his length.

Dammit, my underwear was in the way. We were both dressed way too much to do this properly, but I was a starved woman and would take what he gave me.

As if sensing my need, and since I wasn't being coy, he wedged an arm between us to guide his erection to me. Pushing aside my underwear, he rocked his hips until his shaft was at my entrance.

"Yes," I hissed. He entered and a needy moan escaped. How could I be so close to orgasm in such little time?

He was kissing his way back up my neck. "Natalia," he whispered before he claimed my mouth.

I grasped his shoulders as he set the pace. My keyboard screeched across the desk behind me. My care quotient was low. Anchored to my desk with him dominating my body, I let myself go. Digging my heels into his ass, I held on as he thrust in and out. He pumped up, hitting the most sinful spots inside me. At his deepest point, my clit rubbed against him while my nipples scraped against his shirt.

I moaned and whimpered into his mouth, his strong arms holding me in place.

The force of his thrusts increased, but he kept me from bouncing across the desk.

The first spasm hit and if he weren't wearing a shirt, I would've drawn blood curling my fingernails into him. He pounded into me again, ripping a muffled scream from me.

When the apex of my orgasm hit, I jerked, my legs coming loose from around him, but he held on. He had me. I was safe with him as he swallowed the ecstatic noises I was making and prevented me from falling.

With a final thrust that pushed me higher than I'd ever been, he stiffened and groaned. It was my turn to hold him as he shook with his release. He pulsed inside of me, the moves amplified because my sex was clamped so tightly around him.

We clung to each other as we crashed back to reality.

He didn't jerk away, but he released my mouth and caught my legs to help me down. My breasts spilled out of my top as I sat forward and scooted off the desk.

Oh my god. That just happened. Never in my life had I thought I'd get busy in my office. I stood and let gravity deal with my skirt as I pulled the edges of my shirt together. Looking over my shoulder revealed a few papers hanging off the desk, the keyboard ready to crash to the ground, and the floor littered with stacks that I'd have to reorganize.

It was a strangely satisfying view.

Chris had tucked himself back into his pants and rearranged his shirt. I couldn't meet his eyes as I smoothed my hands over the material that remained bunched over my thighs. I paused as he grasped an edge of my gaping shirt.

"I ruined your top. Do you have something to cover yourself with?"

I nodded. "I have a jacket."

He didn't withdraw his hand but hooked his fingers under my chin and lifted. "We didn't use protection."

I didn't risk dislodging his touch to nod. "I'm still on the pill so I'm not worried. Are you?"

He shook his head, his gaze level. "I just wish…" He sighed and released me to turn away. "I just wish we could've been more."

I had to lean back against the desk again, needing the support. He still wanted to be with me? Beyond our chemistry? "I'm not saying it'd be easy, but we could be." My voice was so small to my own ears.

He swiveled back toward me. "What would you tell your parents about me?"

The question caught me off guard, but it wasn't the reason for my delay in answering. I was running the conversation through my head.

"If you're thinking about how you'd start with my work history before Arcadia, then that's the wrong answer. And honestly, I don't need the detail that I'm fucking the principal thrown in my face when I'm fighting the Richards to parent my own damn kid."

I reared back like he'd slapped me. Didn't he realize the irony of what he'd just said—beyond the hurtful denigration of what we'd just done? "I guess we're done here then."

"Natalia. I didn't mean it like that."

I crossed my arms to help push my shirt together. I was bared enough around him. "No. You said what you meant. You're hung up on what I'd tell my parents, and you're just as afraid our relationship will affect your chances against the Richards. Not to mention the issue of me expelling your daughter." *And having sex in my office.*

"No one can claim you gave us preferential treatment," he said bitterly.

I winced. No. I had. The art project had derailed my intentions, but it'd highlighted another glaring need within the school. And showed I didn't need to come down like Thor's hammer with each infraction.

"Goodbye, Natalia."

He strode out of the room, swinging the door shut behind him. I was enclosed back in my office. Alone—the common factor of all my identities.

hris

"WHAT'S this about Jaycee going to public school?"

I buried my head in the hand that wasn't holding the phone to my ear. The one time Cierra calls Jaycee out of the blue and it's during the school transition. She'd only been expelled two days and would start at the high school in their district tomorrow. "Cierra, that's what I wanted to meet with you for lunch about."

"Mother is going to be pissed, Chris. You promised to send Jaycee to Preston. They paid for everything."

"Did Jaycee tell you what happened? She was with a boy, Cierra."

Silence descended on the other end while I explained each disciplinary action.

"Jaycee mentioned getting in trouble, but didn't mention any of that," Cierra said tersely.

"Honestly, I didn't either because I don't have custody and

I'm afraid your parents are going to take her away. Can you help out with that?" I hadn't meant to be blunt, but Cierra might've called her mother first to complain.

Cierra sighed. "What are they supposed to think? She's sneaking off with boys, changing her appearance, and getting kicked out of freaking school. Something has to change."

"Give her a chance at this new place. Preston wasn't healthy for her."

"Both you and I graduated from there. It's not the school." That was straight up her mother talking. "And I'm getting married at the end of April. I can't deal with this right now."

Did she miss the irony? She claimed the school wasn't a factor in Jaycee's unhappiness, then announced she couldn't deal with Jaycee because of the wedding.

"I'm her father. She's been with me for almost five years. Things were fine until high school started." *Please see the sense in what I'm saying.*

"I'll talk to Mother and Father, but they aren't going to be happy. Without a quality education, they fear for her future."

"Lots of people who succeed in life don't go to Preston Academy."

"Jaycee comes from a legacy."

I held back a snort. They weren't Rockefellers or Vanderbilts. The empire the Richards wanted Jaycee to run was formidable in their mind only. They were good at what they did, and they didn't want to see what they had built die. I couldn't fault them for that. But laying their company's future on a teen wasn't fair. Upsetting her home life to protect it was unreasonable at the least. So was expecting me to sit back while they decided her future and absorbed her into their company. A place she'd be miserable in as she told others how to diversify their portfolios and when they should invest in high-risk stocks.

If that was the future she wanted, then I would support

her. But the only thing Jaycee wanted to invest her time into was her art, helping others with her art and making them happy like she does with Lynne. I seemed to be the only one who knew that about her.

"Why don't we see how she does in public school before we make any permanent decisions?"

"I'm not keeping this a secret from them."

No. It'd ruin her wedding plans. She wanted to shove the problem onto her mommy and daddy and return to her ideal little world.

"About the custody—"

"Chris, now's not the time. I'm. Getting. Married."

"Which makes it the perfect time."

"And do you have money for a lawyer?"

Disappointment coursed through me. "Do we need to go that far?"

"It's a smart move, Chris. I can make all the changes I want, but you should have your own lawyer to read it over."

The lawyer topic had been her stalling tactic when I'd drained my savings to buy a house and open a comic book shop. And I'd gone along with it.

"I have a lawyer." I knew a lawyer. "Are you willing to meet to outline custody arrangements?"

"So not the time. Seriously. Jaycee's been *expelled*."

"Cierra, help me out here." The desperation must've flowed through the phone. She'd called me once upon a time, begging the same way.

"Of course I'll meet with you. You're her father, but we have a serious situation to deal with first."

She probably meant her wedding.

We disconnected and I slumped in my chair with a sigh. I wasn't concerned about getting back to the floor. Mara was arranging displays and since Jaycee wasn't as concerned about her image anymore, she was running the till and helping customers. Going out there to watch her genuinely smile and interact with them was tempting, but I needed a few minutes.

Last night, I'd had to go home and pretend everything was fine, that I hadn't just mauled Natalia in her office after we'd broken up and argued. Then argued again afterward. I'd burned our fajitas and loaded the dishwasher but forgotten to turn it on. Jaycee had teased me about getting old and I couldn't even play it off as a busy day at work because she'd been there.

I rested my head on the back of my chair and stared at the ceiling. My office was the opposite of Mara's. Old movie posters decorated three walls and Jaycee's sketches of the store hung on the fourth wall. The window shade was closed and I let my eyelids drift shut.

I missed Natalia. Spying on her for five seconds before she'd spotted me hadn't helped my control yesterday. The play of the lights over the blond highlights in her hair had caught my eye before my gaze had drifted down to her business-wear-clad ass. She'd had the coat off that went with it—and I'd seen her at work enough to know that the suit coat was a layer to hide behind. Without it, the taper of her waist into the rounded flare of her hips was mesmerizing. Then she'd caught me lusting after her and had barely batted an eye.

But she'd proven she wasn't immune to me either.

What the fuck had we done? Two people who couldn't climb a hill had no business dreaming of mountains—or whatever prophetic words my mom had spewed when I admitted to Cierra's rejection.

I hadn't been able to get the mother of my kid to consider marrying me; I wasn't going to win over Natalia's family.

∽

Natalia

"Henry's on line one," came Ms. Branson's crisp voice through the intercom.

I raised a brow and tore my gaze off the spreadsheet in front of me. Henry must've made his call sound critical. *New week, new mood* had been my motto until Ms. Branson had bypassed our messaging for the intercom. And it was only Monday.

My gaze shifted to the ominous phone. Oh, I knew what the call was about. Frederick Wentworth had gone nuclear when I'd told him Dresden was suspended. The entire board had probably heard his case before the weekend. Coach Sammie had turned beet red and blustered his way straight out of my office and likely right onto Henry's lap to complain about how mean I was.

"Cheater," I muttered. I'd counseled Coach Sammie and expressed that I had one hundred percent confidence in my ability to find a qualified coach who'd hold our students to Preston's standards and not lie for them. I should've fired him, but he was tight with the powerful families who communicated through their pocketbooks. Enraging one family was inconvenient, but I'd be a fool to upset the horde.

I gave the phone one last hard stare and picked it up. "How are you, Henry?"

"I've had better weekends." His tone didn't make my hopes rise.

"I should've notified you what might happen when I started disciplinary action on Jaycee Halliwell and Dresden Wentworth."

"And Coach Samuelson. Look, I'm not interested in a he-said-she-said, especially when my phone kept ringing with more hes and shes." I didn't dare chuckle. Nothing was funny about the situation—but maniacal giggles were fighting to get out. "Based on the claims and accusations, I'm calling an emergency parent meeting tomorrow evening. Six o'clock."

I let my eyelids drift shut. Would I walk into a room with gallows and rotten tomatoes? Henry wasn't interested in excuses. He wasn't a guy who cared to play intermediary between me and upset parents and faculty.

Hanging up with him, my stomach roiled. The meeting was going to be a brutal trial filled with accusations and well-aimed targets about my character. And unlike when Lauren PenaltyCall had tripped me and I'd knocked my head on the floor, I would be hurt and alone.

Chris wasn't going to be around to support me through this mess.

CHAPTER 15

Natalia

I PULLED on my suit jacket. I lined the cuffs up with my sleeves and straightened the bottom. The meeting started in twenty minutes. Henry had arranged for the gathering to take place in the conference room.

My stomach fluttered, harder than last time. I was going to be nauseous by the time the meeting started.

Earlier in the school year, when I'd first arrived, I'd spoken in an auditorium with hundreds of young faces staring at me as I introduced myself and outlined my mission statement and plans for the school. I'd assured them their days wouldn't be disrupted as they restructured minor areas of programming and extracurricular activities.

I had channeled Valaria the whole time.

For the most part, I'd told the truth. Jaycee's and Dresden's actions should've only affected themselves, but the staff that had overlooked the boy's indiscretions had created consequences for the entire student body. What other behavior had been overlooked?

Gazing into the mirror mounted on my wall, I shoved on my freshly cleaned glasses. My hair was bound in my preferred bun, and not one strand dared stray from the fastening. The maroon suit I wore was the perfect color—not too bright and cheerful, but not funereal either.

I'd done nothing wrong.

Or had I? My shoulders slumped, matching the fatigue from sleepless nights in my tired eyes. A sense of failure haunted my steps, and it had started when I'd failed miserably at introducing Chris to my parents.

But my personal life had no place here. I was Ms. Shaw at school, not Natalia Preston Shaw, who clawed at a collapsing slope trying to live up to her parents' expectations.

I stared at myself for several more minutes, pondering where I'd gone wrong. My profession? My personal life? Growing up acquiescing to my parents' wishes? All of the above?

The timer went off on my computer. I spun around and reached over my desk to shut it off. I planned to arrive ten minutes early.

It was time to go.

I left my office and strode out the back door of the main office to get to the conference room. Sneaky like Valaria, or cowardly because walking through the accusing and smug faces of those I dedicated my work to was more than my pride could handle?

No answer was needed.

The clicks of my heels echoed on the floor as I approached my destination. My stomach flipped and I dragged in a ragged breath. Two hours tops and I could go home and drown my sorrows over how it turned out.

I strode through the door. Dresden's parents sat next to

Coach Sammie on the longest side of the rectangular table. Dresden was flanked by his mother and father. Henry was at one end, speaking to Claudia. Douglas, Guy, and Murdock flanked her other side. Henry tipped his head to a chair next to him. Across from the Wentworths was an older couple I didn't recognize. Their regal postures and haughty expressions marked them as Preston grads. Given the Wentworths' presence, I had one guess as to their identities. Nana and Papa.

I swallowed hard, adopted a stern face, and strutted to the chair.

Silence descended in the room. The burn of their stares pounded into me. I settled in my chair and dared to lift my gaze.

I sat on Henry's right side, lessening the feeling of being on trial. Avoiding their gazes, I quickly scanned the room. It was too small to have missed Chris or Jaycee. Neither one was present.

A figure turned into the doorway, his broad form filling out the opening. He cut a fine form in his charcoal tailored suit, and he would've had to tailor it for his size and width. Chris's borderline shaggy hair was now neatly trimmed, parted on one side, and combed across his forehead. His style was professional, yet contemporary and relevant. He could be walking straight out of a *GQ* magazine cover into the conference room.

His gaze lifted to meet mine. The gravity in his eyes told me all I needed to know about how things were going in his life since Jaycee had been expelled.

But why was he here? To petition for his daughter's return? Or to help launch an attack on me?

Hurt wound its way into my heart. Either way, we were adversaries now.

Two hours. I clung to that thought. I would be at home in

my bed and could cry if I needed to. I dropped my gaze from Chris as he lowered himself into the chair opposite Henry. He straightened his silver-patterned tie, and god, it was unfair that he'd shown up looking that good.

Yeah, I'd probably need a good sob.

Henry muttered, "We'd better start on time." He cleared his throat and captured everyone's attention. "Welcome. Thank you all for coming. As you know, meeting the needs of our students as they develop into future leaders is our priority. We've gone through a period of changes after we discovered some unsavory behavior from a man we previously trusted with the role of guiding our students and staff, changes that we entrusted to Ms. Shaw to direct. But it's been brought to our attention this has resulted in conflict and grievous accusations."

Heads bobbed in the audience. I snuck a peek at Chris, but his gaze was directed at Henry.

Henry continued. "Let me say before we get started that the board and I won't hesitate to dismiss anyone who acts in a less than appropriate manner. What the board wants to hear is serious complaints about the professional decisions Ms. Shaw has made and how you think they have negatively impacted the student body. Please, no interruption from those waiting to talk."

My respect for Henry grew. If he could keep the meeting on track, then maybe I wouldn't be so figuratively bruised and battered by the time I got home.

Dresden's dad leaned across the table, his tweed suit coat stretching over his shoulders. "My son has experienced a personal, targeted attack from Ms. Shaw. He's had to do detention, now he's been suspended, and after he's contributed his time morning and night to bring the Preston Knights another trophy."

I was running through ways of addressing the accusations

without dragging Dresden and Jaycee's dirty laundry out in front of people who didn't know the situation when Claudia spoke.

"Would you mind telling us why you feel it's personal? Ms. Shaw has provided the necessary documentation and proof that her actions were warranted."

Mr. Wentworth's upper lip curled and his dark gaze pierced her. "Because she's dating the father of the girl she said Dresden allegedly skipped with."

Ice crystals formed in my veins. Had he really waved my personal life around? I didn't have to wonder how he knew. Jaycee must've either let it slip or she had gleefully spread the news after the breakup.

The heads of all five members of the board swiveled to face me. I looked down the length of the table, my gaze steady. Show no fear. It might be one of Valaria's mottos, but it worked here. Pretend I'd done nothing wrong even if I felt differently.

"Like Claudia said, I documented the reasons behind my decisions for your son's disciplinary measures, and while I won't go into specifics about another student, I will add that the girl you referenced also faced consequences for her role in the tardiness and skipping."

Mr. Wentworth's cheeks deepened to a red, highlighting what was the main problem in my opinion. The man wasn't told no very often. Between his bank account, his size, the consulting company he owned, and even the solid dose of charm guys like him were born with, he was a man people wanted to please.

The woman I suspected was Nana lifted her hand almost like she was going to request to speak.

Henry lifted his chin to her. Mr. Wentworth eased back into his chair, but we weren't done hearing from him. His body language was too tense, and his wife was shooting him "fix this" daggers in her gaze.

Nana's hand went to her chest. She wore a crisp lilac pantsuit with a taupe shawl draped across her neck, and her no-nonsense expression said she could probably go toe to toe with Mr. Wentworth if they weren't on the same side.

"That girl," the woman said, her voice firmer than she looked, "is my granddaughter, who was expelled after my granddaughter's father broke up with *Ms. Shaw*." Venom dripped from my name.

My face burned. My personal life was getting thrown around and the meeting was going worse than I'd imagined.

A stifled sigh escaped Henry and I could almost hear him mentally yelling, "You could've warned me."

On the bright side, I only had to experience the humiliation of the big reveal of my privacy once.

"The two are exclusive," I said. Truly, one didn't have to do with the other. "Ms. Richards?" The woman nodded. "I can also provide proper documentation and evidence that would back up my decision, along with citing the relevant Preston Academy policies regarding student punishments. However, I can only discuss school-related material with you. Anything regarding the student in question can only be discussed with her guardian, which to my knowledge is not you."

Ms. Richards recoiled. The hit was below the belt and I knew it, but I got enough shit from parents and guardians. Entitled grandparents were not on my list of people I had to put up with. I chanced a glance at Chris.

His eyes had closed and his mouth was flat. Damn. I'd made it worse for him.

Mr. Richards put an arm around his wife. His graying hair was smartly styled like Chris's, but he won the most casually dressed award in the room. The man would blend well on a golf course with his gray slacks and white polo.

"We paid Jaycee's tuition. We're invested in her education—she's a third-generation Preston student. While we may not be her official guardians *yet*, we are heavily invested in her education."

I winced. Chris cut a glare in the direction of the Richards. How could a good dad lose his daughter?

Henry cleared his throat. "When the paperwork is official, we'll be happy to discuss your granddaughter's return with you."

My eyes widened and I swiveled to look at Henry. Chris was in the room and these people were talking about his daughter's future like he was insignificant. None of them knew Jaycee like her own father.

Henry had my documentation of the incidents, but he didn't know Jaycee. Coming back here would be a move backward for her development. She might mentally shut down, act out again, maybe let another boy use her emotions to his benefit.

Claudia blinked at Henry, her gaze shifting to Chris. Murdock did the same. They didn't know the lack of power Chris faced. Maybe they assumed he was giving up on his daughter like her mom had.

Henry returned my stunned gaze with a hard stare. He wasn't my ally. He wasn't Jaycee's either. The big picture for the academy was his focus, and the Richards were regular donors.

Chris's voice caught my attention. He was sitting straight, his hands folded on the table, looking like he ruled the boardroom. I could envision him on a poster that wouldn't have to say "vote for me" because I'd want to anyway based off the picture he presented.

"Two days after Jaycee was kicked out"—he briefly met

my gaze, then looked each board member in the eyes—"she started at the high school in our school district. The transition hasn't been easy, but her excitement and optimism every day has been enough to tell me we're on the right track. No matter what her mother and I decide, I don't think Jaycee returning to Preston is in her best interest."

Mr. Richards's face flushed red. "You're coming to Ms. Shaw's defense even now?"

"I'm here for Jaycee."

Mrs. Richards's words were low, but they carried across the room. "Not when we're done with you. A comic book shop owner is not raising our granddaughter."

My back hit my chair. They were going to yank a girl from her father because of this fucking school? A place that made no apologies for failing her? Jaycee couldn't even leave now that she'd refused to conform to Preston's mentality.

Perhaps Jaycee still had a way out.

I had never gotten the opportunity to attend a different school. All along, I'd kept my private life and my personal one strictly separate. Why? I wanted to have a life, period. But I'd been trained like one of my parents' staff to do their bidding, to think pleasing them equated with love and acceptance. All of it done under the guise of professionalism and leadership.

I spoke before I could think about what I was doing. "You're right. I did let my relationship with Mr. Halliwell affect how I treated Jaycee." Mrs. Richards's eyes narrowed like she was looking for the catch. "Instead of suspending her and sending her out of my office, per Preston policy, I did something I don't normally do with students—I listened."

A faint smile graced Chris's mouth, giving me the motivation to keep going.

"And you see, I think that's what this school has been

failing at. I think that's the root cause of the problems that prompt someone like me to come here in the first place."

Coach Samuelson snorted. "Aren't you here because you're the owner's daughter?"

The room went silent.

"I'm here because my father wanted me to take over for him, and I've kept my ties to the school quiet because I knew any progress I made would be undermined by being 'just the boss's daughter.' Of course, any mistakes would result in the same accusations. Kinda like how dating Chris was tossed into this discussion."

"For good reason," Mr. Wentworth said. "But I don't see what that has to do with letting the kids run the place."

Chris jumped in before I could. "Listening to kids and letting them have free rein are two different things. Jaycee wasn't happy here and Natalia asked her why."

I couldn't flinch at his informality. Him not calling me Ms. Shaw was a victory. "This educational system was designed around what a specific set of parents wanted for their kids—*decades* ago. I've never stopped to ask what the kids thought they needed to prepare for adulthood. They're the ones associating with other kids who've had more exposure to what's available beyond Preston. Many area public schools have technology labs. We don't have more than five iPads in the building. Why *don't* we consult the kids? They have more ideas than we give them credit for. Wait, I know the answer. Like you pointed out, Coach, it's because I was one of those kids. No choice. No other interests allowed. Now, I'm an adult, and I'm finding this damn school still dictates what I should and shouldn't like." *Who* I should like. "I'm done with it."

The epiphany hit me. I hadn't said that for effect. I was done with it.

Blinking, I looked up at Chris. The whole room was watching me, but I focused on him. "I quit."

"Ms. Shaw—" Henry said.

"No. I do. I quit. But you know what? I can walk away—finally! Jaycee can't. She needs her parents and I've only seen one take an active interest in her life. Coincidently, he's the only one here. I wish my father had taken a personal interest in me. Half the time"—ninety-nine percent—"I feel like the only purpose behind my birth was to run these oppressive, misogynistic, dictatorial schools, and I let it ruin all the good things in my life."

Mr. Richards's eyebrows dropped over his eyes. "Now listen here—"

I pushed back. "Nope. Not my problem anymore. Henry, I'm cleaning out my office."

I rose and swept out of the room without looking back at Chris. The sight of him might've bolstered me or dropped me. Because my newfound sense of self had come two months too late.

On my way to my office, the *click-click* of my heels sounding as desperate for escape as I felt, I texted my parents.

I quit Preston. I refuse to be affiliated with this school. Call you when I have time.

No doubt one of the board members or the Richards was already dialing my father.

They were going to disown me. My trust fund was mine, but even if they found a way to leave me penniless, I'd make a living. I was a legit teacher, after all. Many schools would be grateful to hire a former principal as a teacher.

Right?

God, I didn't know. I knew no one in the field. Would I have to move back to Seattle?

Go where the jobs were. No one was tying me here.

Tears pricked the backs of my eyes. No one was waiting for me anywhere.

I stifled a sob and rushed into my office. The sooner I was packed, the sooner I could skim help-wanted ads and call moving companies.

∽

Chris

As Natalia disappeared around the corner, I picked up the pace. I wasn't going to charge after her like a madman. But it was hard to convince myself not to.

I'd just told Cierra's parents to stay out of my and Cierra's business and walked out of the meeting. Natalia was right. Preston Academy was designed for one reason, and who was I to say they were wrong?

But as Jaycee's father, he could say, *nope, my daughter is going to school where she chooses.* She'd go where she fell in with a group of friends who cared about her and not with a boy who cared about nailing her virginity.

I would go down broke and swinging on that account.

Ahead, what sounded like a sob spurred me to go faster. She had stepped into her office and was swinging the door shut behind her.

I rushed inside and closed the door.

She turned with a gasp, her arm drawing back.

Holding up my hands, I leaned against the door. "Easy with the Krav Maga."

"I've only taken a self-defense course."

I grinned. "Good. Could you teach Jaycee?"

She chuckled and we both fell quiet.

"I'm sorry—"

"What a shit show," I said over her.

"Yeah. It has been for a while. But I'm sorry."

I shrugged. "You were doing your job, even if the mentality here sucks. If it had been the last principal, he'd have let Dresden keep running off with my girl, and she'd have stayed with him because she was miserable. Then there'd be a fourth-generation Preston kid."

Another laugh burst out of her. "Sounds awful." Her smile faded. "Is she really doing well?"

I pushed off the door. "No exaggeration. The first day, some kids saw her sketches and now she's snap-whatevering them all freaking day. She even shows them to me. Do you know how many drawing apps there are?"

A flash of a grin faded. "I'd love to know. I'd love to hear her stories and see her work."

I drifted closer. Tension vibrated through me like a tuning fork. "Well, I happened to hear you're not busy later. Want to come over?"

"I'm so not busy now." The sound she made was a mix of a laugh and a cry. "Why would you want me over?"

"Are you serious? After I witnessed Shaw Shank slap down an entire room of esteemed Preston Academy faculty and donors?"

"I didn't do anything but quit. And text my parents about it." She screwed up her face. "My phone is going to vibrate apart, but I told them I'd call them later."

I whistled low. "Shit's serious now."

She considered me, her head tilting to the side, one hand running along my lapel. "I want for it to be serious again. I'll even send my father a selfie of us and hash tag it 'ownsatoystore.'"

She'd told off the school board, left her job, and notified her parents right away? I hadn't met this Natalia yet. Or had I? The real Natalia had ripped her mask off.

I lifted her glasses off her face and tossed them in the trash. Her lips twitched.

Cupping her cheek, I said, "You can tell them that they can get the friends and family discount if they shop at Arcadia."

Her laughter—it'd been too long since I'd heard it. And too soon it was gone. "What are you going to do about Jaycee?"

The corner of my mouth kicked up. "We had a long talk about her future and her authority over it. She's with her mom now and I fully expect Nana and Papa are going to get an earful."

"They don't seem like the type of people who'll listen."

"Her mother might. The peace of Cierra's wedding is at stake."

"Devious."

I hadn't moved my hand, and she rubbed her cheek against it. "We're preparing for war. You met Ephraim at the party. Our store uses his law firm for all things legal and he has a contact for me if the Richards try to interfere with custody. I have some assets I can cash in for the retainer. But mostly, Jaycee and I are hoping they don't call our bluff."

"I hope you don't have to do that." We were chest to chest.

"It's past due."

"I know a former principal of a prestigious private school who can vouch for your character."

"I don't think it'll go over well once I tell them just how unprofessional our relationship is." I lowered my head. This time, after we repeated the desk episode, I would leave with her on my arm.

ix months later…
Chris

I WANDERED the perimeter of the trade show floor. Once again, Arcadia got the primo corner booth and we'd outdone even last year's showing. Six-foot renditions of popular comics lined the wall behind the tables. We had pull boxes for comic books and action figure displays arranged on the corners.

Twenty minutes and the doors to the Twin Cities Comic Con would open. A line outside had already formed around the building. Even though I was a fanboy and had waited in line for comic cons, it still humbled me that others wanted to come to spend the weekend at an event I had put hours of energy into.

"Hey, Dad." Jaycee straightened from behind the booth where she was helping Mara shuffle boxes of action figures and brochures under the table. "Do you want me to stock the little TARDIS key chains, too?"

"Sure, if there's room." A smile tickled my lips as Jaycee eyed the table.

Her cosplay costume was homemade. Every hour Jaycee and Natalia spent hunched over the sewing machine was better than any movie I could watch. They laughed and joked and put me to work ironing fabric.

Full custody was a heady prospect. Jaycee still spent one weekend, or at least part of it, with her grandparents. Cierra had invited her over a few times for a sleepover. Best of all, I had less to do with all of them than when Jaycee had gone to Preston. We all tolerated each other, having come to an agreement after the Preston debacle last spring. Nana and Papa weren't willing to run Jaycee out of their lives by fighting for custody, and Cierra had actually listened to Jaycee and not isolated herself to keep the drama from affecting her precious wedding.

The rumble of wheels on the floor sounded behind me.

"Excuse me. I'm in need of a superhero, but I don't know who you are."

I spun around, trying not to be self-conscious in my skintight gray superhero suit. Shaw Shank's hands were on her hips, a wicked grin on her face. A black star was painted over her right eye, but it didn't prevent her from being recognizable.

"I have a special surprise for attendees who know who I am," I said, tapping the blue emblem on my chest. Nightwing.

Natalia skated closer and dropped her voice. "What if I were to admit that I know who you really are, I just like to hear you get defensive."

I held out my hand and pulled her closer. "I'll have to deal with you later." I gave her a quick kiss.

"Half my class said they were going to come today." Excitement vibrated in her voice.

"Extra credit or they didn't believe you could roller skate?"

She tapped my arm. "You know I don't give extra credit."

I laughed. Natalia had embraced her real self but being a strict teacher with high expectations was a part of her.

After only a couple months as a Family and Consumer Science middle school teacher, Jaycee had heard stories that Natalia was tough but well-liked by her students. Part of her relatability in FACS was that she was learning with the students. Her sewing skills had landed her the job, but with her first class, she'd announced that they would all learn how to cook from the students in each class who already had the skills.

It was a win for everybody, especially for me. Jaycee was blossoming into a fun teenager to be around. Natalia had moved in—movie night every weekend. My parents had loved her. Hers… They were trying, and that was more than Natalia and I thought they'd do.

She rolled into me for another kiss. "I'd better get back to the Mean Streaks' booth."

"I have it on good authority there'll be a sexy assassin sneaking around tomorrow."

Her saucy smile was dangerous to a guy in a superhero suit. I couldn't wait for the next day. Valaria wasn't retired. Instead of taking the time to design a new cosplay identity, Natalia had helped a couple of students make their own. I didn't know who was more excited, Natalia or the kids.

I loved the enthusiastic FACS teacher as much as I loved Ms. Shaw, Valaria, and Shaw Shank. Each identity was all a part of Natalia Shaw and they were no longer secret, or separate, and I was crazy for every part of her.

I'd love to know what you thought. Please consider leaving a review for First to Fail at the retailer the book was purchased from.

For all the latest news, sneak peeks, quarterly short stories, and free material sign up for my newsletter.

ABOUT THE AUTHOR

Marie Johnston writes paranormal and contemporary romance and has collected several awards in both genres. Before she was a writer, she was a microbiologist. Depending on the situation, she can be oddly unconcerned about germs or weirdly phobic. She's also a licensed medical technician and has worked as a public health microbiologist and as a lab tech in hospital and clinic labs. Marie's been a volunteer EMT, a college instructor, a security guard, a phlebotomist, a hotel clerk, and a coffee pourer in a bingo hall. All fodder for a writer!! She has four kids and even more cats.

mariejohnstonwriter.com

Follow me: